Advance Praise

I've never read a more powerful anti-war novel than The Battle for Snow Mountain, not that it is an anti-war novel in an ideological sense or a political novel. The reader shares the fact that no one knew what was going on, the blinding snowstorms working beautifully. There is the quixotic pair, idealistic and realistic, but again, not as symbols, but as real people.

The letters to the family are an imaginative stroke because they convey the family's incomprehension about what war is like. And Gloria (like Dulcinea in *Don Quixote*) is amusing and attractive. The poems which reflect on the scenes, (written by Richard) are lovely and imaginative, contrasting with the absurdity of war. The final liberation is beautifully done.

-John Dizikes, formerly Professor in the
American Studies Program at the University
of California, Santa Cruz.

The Battle for Snow Mountain was very enjoyable to read. To me, the main characters, Richard and Timmons portray the best of America that was sent to defeat evil. The idealistic poet and the negative wise guy both had similar paths in the War but very different views about it. One loses his glasses and can't quite see what it is he is part of; the other loses his faith, even though he also acted like he never had any in the first place. The conflicted feelings that Richard felt as he journeyed home seemed so real to me. He is going to get a hero's welcome back home, but he feels as if he failed in battle and doesn't quite know how to react to it. When his father requests that he not tell anyone the unpleasant details of his service, I thought that was the worst thing he could do! So many men kept too many things bottled up after the War.

-Craig Bardell, Director of the National World War II Museum in New Orleans, LA.

The Battle
for Snow Mountain

Donald J. Young

Pocol Press
Clifton, VA

POCOL PRESS

Published in the United States of America
by Pocol Press.
6023 Pocol Drive
Clifton, VA 20124
http://www.pocolpress.com

Publisher's Cataloguing-in-Publication

Young, Donald J. (Donald Jorden), 1923-

    The battle for Snow Mountain / Donald J.
    Young. -- Clifton, VA : Pocol Press, c2011.

        p. ; cm.

        ISBN: 978-1-929763-48-1

        1. Ardennes, Battle of the, 1944-1945--Fiction.
2. World War, 1939-1945--Fiction. 3. Prisoners of war--
Germany--Fiction. 4. World War, 1939-1945--France--
Fiction. 5. Historical fiction. I. Title.

PS3575.O7828 B38 2011

[Fic]--dc22   1104

We see our lives reflected either in an idealistic or

realistic mirror.

"Eisenhower admitted error in not considering that Hitler would mount an offensive."

A quote about the massive German breakthrough in the Ardennes woods in the winter of 1944 – from *World War II A 50th Anniversary History,* Henry Holt and Company, 1989.

To Viviane

For all her love and support

I want to thank Harry Card and Evelyn Volpa for their invaluable assistance in editing and preparing the novel for publication.

Jenny Petter is the excellent graphic artist who created the cover.

Mike De Boer took the author photograph.

At the Front

1

Richard couldn't see anything in the morning snowfall, which was so much like the heavy rising fog he couldn't tell them apart. He heard the ominous rumbling of what might be German artillery guns, sounding like distant bowling pins crashing down.

A few GIs began digging holes, like scared animals, though their holes quickly filled up with melting snow and they had to give up their efforts.

Richard had a time fitting his tall frame into a ditch he'd chosen for protection against any artillery rounds. His horn-rimmed glasses, pushed down by the heavy steel helmet, kept sliding down his nose. They'd also fogged up from the cold.

He had a book under his shirt, his small book of love poems. Yet he hadn't been able to read, his eyes weary from lack of sleep. If anyone spoke to him he gave the impression he was sleeping.

He was amazed they'd actually come to the front. He felt he now had a chance for important action in the combat to come.

The Sergeant didn't know where they were, except that they were somewhere in Germany's Snow Mountain, and the Captain wouldn't come up on the line to enlighten them about their positions. He was hiding like a mole in the network of ditches at the rear outpost, shaking at the slightest rustle of a branch in the woods.

What an effort it had been, Richard thought, moving thousands of men of the Lion Division into Germany in the dark, like easing cattle off a road into the snow of unfamiliar woods. For days they'd driven across France, telling jokes in the back of the truck like boy scouts, singing "Roll me over in the clover," forgetting for a moment they were going to the front. Groaner, a short, weepy Tennessean with an old man's face, one of the recent "casualty replacements," had taken out a small banjo that he'd hidden under his heavy winter coat and sang, to his own plucking accompaniment, a song about an abandoned hillbilly.

"No letter today, no letter from home," he droned on. "I've waited since dawn, no letter from home."

A few hummed along with Groaner but halfway through his performance he began weeping and since he didn't have a barracks post handy he banged his head against the side of the banjo. A GI shouted at him to stop blubbering, grabbed the instrument and passed it like a ball to the guy at the rear of the truck – Groaner yelling to get it back until it was handed to him with a string busted and a chip in the side of the wood.

The Germans, they said, were just a few hundred yards from them, down in the valley. Richard tried to dig deeper in his trench but it filled up with slush from the snow below the surface. He didn't feel like covering himself with his sleeping bag. He'd feel naked with just a woolen cover between him and a German on patrol.

The blinding snow made a screen between him and the Germans – he couldn't see them and they couldn't see him. The wind whipped his face, showering him with powder snow from the screen of evergreens. He had never known such bone-chilling cold. It reminded him of the deep-freeze locker on his family's farm in Bethlehem, which he'd lean into, to pull out a side of beef.

When the word passed around that it was chow time Richard left his ditch to take a place in the line of GIs. It was ominous that the soldiers, since they got off the trucks, had lost their singing mood and were quiet as mice, not even talking about the food they were getting.

He was so bogged down by his wet brown overcoat and belt of grenades that he could hardly budge. It was around noon, he figured, but with the screen of snow, he still had trouble seeing. As he stepped over a pile of snow, swaying like an acrobat, he tripped over his long scarf and stumbled against a GI, who said, "Screw you!" in a shrill voice.

The chow line passed in front of four small metal cans. Supervising the operation was Catton, the cook – a bald, hard-faced man who never spoke, wiping his hands on his apron as if he'd just prepared a meal in their Georgia camp. Amazing, Richard thought, to be eating a banquet just a few hundred yards from the enemy.

He took his tin plate and moved forward, stepping on GIs who were eating while lying down in the snow, their bodies forming a thick unstable carpet. Meat, vegetables and ice cream were piled onto his plate.

He sat down against a tree near his friend, Timmons, who was sprawled out in the snow, his belt hanging loose, his wool cap pulled down under his helmet, looking like furry ears. They'd known each other in high school but had only become friends when they were inducted into service together. And so far they'd remained together in the same infantry company.

Timmons had been a football star in high school, with a short body, a huge head as hard as stone. When he bashed into the opponent's line he'd scatter the tackles, injuring them, and they'd complain, as if his head was an illegal weapon, like a boxer's fist. He himself had a permanently bruised right cheekbone from helmets smashing into his face.

Richard recalled that his friend had a reputation in high school for going out every Saturday night to the south side of Bethlehem, the slum area, where he'd pick up a prostitute. The other guys tried to shame him for this, feeling slightly jealous of his prowess in this sexual arena, an unknown world to them.

His fellow students thought Timmons often made dumb remarks but occasionally came up with a striking comment that surprised them. They didn't know if he was mentally slow (his elevator didn't go to the top floor) or whether he simply played dumb (dumb as a fox).

Eating his meal he turned to Richard, "I guess we're going into combat now. And the Captain's afraid to come up to the front."

3

"He's probably needed back there."

"I doubt it. He's chicken. And I've been talking to some of the veterans in our outfit. It's not going to be any picnic for us."

"That makes it more of a challenge. When we get back they'll stand up when we walk into a room."

"I doubt it. And you know these guys in our company haven't the foggiest idea what's going on."

"I think they believe in what they're doing. You need to read history, Timmons. We're fighting Hitler who killed millions of Jews in his own country."

"Why did the Germans let him do it?"

"They didn't have any control over him."

"They elected him."

"He seized power. Timmons, you got to read history."

"I still say – why did ordinary Germans go along with him?"

"They had to follow orders."

"Like we're doing. We're here to kill German boys who had nothing to do with Hitler. They're not our enemies."

"Timmons, they *are* our enemies."

"Richard, I have to tell you something that's bothering me."

"What's that?"

"I don't know if I can actually kill someone."

"You have to or he'll kill you."

"But what if I can't do it?"

"You should've applied at the Induction Center as a conscientious objector. But then you had to prove you were a churchgoer."

"I'm not a churchgoer. But if I run into a German soldier tomorrow, how do I know I can kill him? I've never killed anyone before."

"Well, we're in a holy war now."

"I bet they say that in every war."

Timmons was trying to forget their division was totally untrained for any mission. The outfit was made up of men recently taken from school or from the air corps. They were all

4

walking blindly through a land of snow, ripe for a catastrophe.

The next day while on a morning patrol Richard heard voices coming from the bottom of a nearby ravine and he froze. He listened, concentrating. In a few minutes he heard someone speaking English and he slowly stumbled down an embankment and stepped through a curtain of trees. There, men from his Company were sitting in a half circle around a tall, angular, rugged man wearing starched fatigues, peeling potatoes. Two men stood around him, in civvies: one taking notes, the other snapping photographs of the tall guy. Beyond a hedgerow was a Red Cross jeep that had brought the visitor to the front.

Richard stared at the man leaning against the tree, carving up spuds. There was something familiar about him. He must be somebody famous, wearing fatigues as a disguise.

At the photographer's request the man turned his head and Richard thought the man looked like Joe DiMaggio. He retraced his steps and called up to Timmons, "Hey, I think it's Joe DiMaggio."

Timmons ran down the bank to join him and Richard pushed his way through to the inner circle. The famous athlete held up a potato and said, "I expect to get a medal of honor for this."

Everyone laughed except Richard. He wondered – was he really the great slugger? And why would they bring him up to the front and risk his life? He remembered how DiMaggio had saved the Yankees last season, coming out of a hospital bed to lead them to victory. He'd just put his bat out and pushed the ball into center field, scoring the winning run and sending them into the World Series.

Richard had seen Gehrig once. His father had taken him to a World Series game as a birthday present. It was late in the Iron Man's career. On his way to the plate Gehrig passed their box and Richard's father waved at him and he waved back. When he came to bat he struck out for the third time that day. Nobody cared. This was Ruth's prince, a massive man like a carved statue, whose sloppy baggy pants made Richard think he had an enormous rear.

Suddenly Timmons wanted to talk to this famous athlete. He might have some answers for him. He raised his hand. "Can I ask a question, Joe?"

The correspondent began to write on his white pad. The photographer focused his camera.

"I'm not trying to be a smart-ass," Timmons said, "but why are you peeling potatoes?" The two civilians laughed.

"Seriously," Timmons said. "You're the greatest. What are you doing here? You're taking a chance, you know."

"I'm just doing my duty," the man said. "I was ordered by the USO to fly up here and they put me on KP."

Everyone chuckled again; the correspondent exploded with laughter.

"They fly a VIP up here," Timmons said, "take pictures of him and make people back home think it's all a picnic. Joe, you shouldn't be at the front. But I got a question for you. I played some college ball. What do you do when you're in a slump? Maybe you're with a team that's lost its nerve. You don't think you're going to make it."

"You just keep coming up to bat," the man said.

"Yeah," Timmons said. "You know, I saw a picture of you once with a gun on your shoulder. You were holding up a pheasant you'd just shot. You know, nobody in our outfit has ever fired his gun. Come with us. I'll ask the Sergeant. You at least could shoot somebody."

"Sure," the popular figure said. "You ask him."

"Did you hear that?" Timmons said to the other GIs, "DiMag might come with us."

"Timmons," the Sergeant shouted down from the top of the ravine. "Haul your ass up here. We're going to assemble."

Timmons put out his hand. "Goodbye," he said. The man took his hand and shook it. "I know it's not your fault," he

6

went on. "They take a guy like myself and try to make a fighter out of him and they take a great shot like you and have him peel potatoes."

"Come on, Timmons," the Sergeant called down, "or you'll get your ass peeled."

He started to leave, then turned around. "Hey, Joe. How about showing us your swing? One for the road."

The famous personage hesitated, then got up. The reporter began scratching his pad. The photographer held his camera ready like a gun. The athlete took his stance, holding an imaginary bat on his shoulder, his body straight as an elm, his feet planted wide; and then he swung furiously, with the camera clicking, in a beautiful wide arc.

"Yeah," Timmons said, moving off slowly, pleased as were the grinning GIs from the Company. From the top of the bank he shouted down, "Joe, remember – if you want to join us, it's I Company, the 506th. Ask anybody for the most fucked-up outfit in the Ardennes forest."

"Come on, Timmons," the Sergeant said, in his grating voice.

"It was DiMaggio," he replied.

"Sure it was," the Sergeant said, with a grin. "Come on, fellow. Whoever it was, he doesn't give a turd in hell about you."

A cloud of fog was blown over them by a gust of wind. To rejoin the company Timmons had to climb a wire fence, being careful to keep from sliding off into the deep snow. He swung his foot up and over the top, climbing down the other side and easing to the ground so his pack wouldn't slide off. Every bush that crackled under him, every limb that swished as he held it up and let it fly back, scared him. Germans were everywhere in the woods, they said, dressed up like GIs to fool them.

He had to dump and in such circumstances little things were great hurdles for him. Not being practical he had to do his business by the numbers. He unslung his gas mask – the others had long ago tossed theirs away – set his pack down, took out

7

his shovel and dug a hole. He put his right hand down to balance himself like a fullback waiting for the ball. Edging toward the fence he straddled the hole, his eyes glazed over like he was under hypnosis. Just a few feet from his head a branch lined with snow was brushed aside by the wind like a curtain and he made out the profile of a soldier, buried in a helmet that had the odd slit of the German fashion. Two more grey figures walked into view, then the three moved on. No longer frozen by his fear Timmons finished his job, kicked dirt over his mess like a dog, re-armed himself and moved back over the fence. Terror that had stopped his movement had saved him.

After they all got back to the campsite at midday the Sergeant came up to explain their position. Red-faced from the wind, seemingly blown up by his thick woolen coat, he moved his huge body through the snow carefully like a dancer, sure of his divine purpose – that God was putting him on trial, leading him into combat with an untrained division.

"Listen, you Johnnies, gather around," he ordered.

The wind blew snow into their faces, the flakes striking their skin like hail, freezing their cheeks, chilling their heavy coats and pants.

Rule and his friend Rabbit stared at the map laid out on the table of snow. They looked forward to action – the only two who could shoot a gun with any precision since they'd been hunters – Rabbit in Pennsylvania, Rule in Virginia. They'd spent hours discussing guns and how to track down their prey. Richard had tried to get friendly with Rule, a proud, reserved fellow, stocky and handsome but he admitted only Rabbit to his private musings on guns and hunting. Rabbit, a short GI with a childish smile, was a better shot than Rule – never missed his bird, he said with conviction. He would, if he ever had a chance, hit his German. He had already gone out on a private patrol but the fog had prevented him from drawing an accurate bead on one of the shadowy figures in the woods. The Sergeant had bawled him out for wandering off but Rabbit mollified the noncom by telling him the lay of the terrain, how to investigate the nearby woods, and how to come back to the camp the easiest way.

"Here's the setup," the Sergeant said to the assembled GIs. "If you can't see the map, I'll pass it around later. Here's the road we took coming from Belgium into Snow Mountain. On the northwest tip you see this town of Losheim. There's a long winding valley here called The Losheim Gap. In every war the Germans have broken through this region. The only way their tanks can get to us is through Stein. So we're going to attack that town and see what's going on. If the Germans are in the valley we have to launch our offensive and put our finger in the gap."

Richard stared at the map. In Basic he'd been fascinated by maps, the intricate moves of men and machines across fields, down into valleys, from hedgerow to hedgerow and into the great woods. He trusted maps – they kept things in order like math, his favorite subject. Now he was on safe ground. With the map he could figure out what was happening. They could outwit the enemy with a clever ploy.

"Where are we?" he asked the Sergeant.

"We're somewhere southwest of Stein."

"Where are the Germans?" Rabbit asked.

"We're not sure," the Sergeant said. "Intelligence says they're heading south. But there may be German units across from us. That's what we're supposed to find out."

"If there's a build-up in the Gap," Timmons said, "we're going to run into trouble."

"I did some reconnoitering," Rabbit said. "I saw this black flag waving from a turret, where German soldiers were walking back and forth."

"There are Germans down there all right," the Sergeant said. "We just don't know how many."

9

"What about aerial reconnaissance?" Richard asked.

"Our planes can't fly through the snow," the Sergeant said.

"You guys don't know anything," Groaner said. "You sit around your map like a bunch of Napoleons. You don't even know where we are. You don't know where we're going. We'll be wiped out like sheep – wait and see."

"Groaner," the Sergeant said, "if I catch you singing any of your weepy songs, I'll give you something to sing about."

"Sergeant," Timmons said, "if there are Germans down there, wouldn't it be better if we could shoot them before they shoot us?"

"Yeah."

"Then why haven't we ever fired our new guns?"

"You'll have a chance to fire your gun soon enough."

"You mean, when I run into a German, I have to shoot and zero in my M-1 at the same time?"

"You got it, Timmons. You know, you play dumb. All through Basic I had to listen to you, always giving that goddamn Tarzan yell of yours – Yahooooo."

The tech Smiley, the Sergeant's genial buddy and assistant, came out of the woods to join them. "I just talked to the Captain," he said.

"Why isn't he up here?" the Sergeant asked.

"He says he's needed at the rear to manage the phones," Smiley said.

"He's shitting in his pants and nothing's happened yet," Timmons said.

The men looked at Smiley for reassurance – a mild-mannered ex-mechanic, with a thin mustache, a gentle noncom out of place in combat fatigues, friendly to the GIs, mothering them. "Listen, you guys," he said. "The Captain just got word from Battalion Headquarters. We're in luck. The Germans are definitely going south. They hit a whole bunch of our guys on the southern flank. But we'll just sit here for the rest of the war and enjoy our Christmas packages from home. There's nothing for you guys to worry about. We'll get accustomed to combat the easy way."

"I'm not afraid," Rule said. "I don't care if there's a hundred Panzer units down there."

"I'm anxious to bag me a few Germans," Rabbit said.

"Big talk," Groaner said.

"What about the fog?" Timmons asked the Sergeant. "How can we attack a town we can't see?"

"We'll walk north till we run into it," the Sergeant said. "But we're going to find that misbegotten town of Stein and blow it away. Now you guys settle in and keep it quiet. The Colonel will tell us when we're going to attack."

Attack, Timmons thought. The word was like the bell before one of his boxing matches in high school. He noticed that he was sweating under his jacket, even in the bitter cold. Suddenly a whirling rush of sound shattered the air over his head, like nothing he'd ever heard before and he was down in the deep snow. He had hit the earth by reflex, propelled by the blast into a ditch, his body rigid. He was amazed how his reflexes had taken over and spun him to the ground. He hadn't heard any distant sound of a shell going off, to connect with the sudden whirring of the mad bird that tore the air above his head. Another shell whizzed over him and he froze; then another screamed by and exploded not far from him, spraying snow into the air, which dropped down like a snowfall – followed by a cry from a nearby field. Timmons squirmed in his ditch; another shell blasted over him and he gritted his teeth, saying, "No, no, no."

The shelling ended and he stood up, feeling stupid. His gun was clogged with snow. The other GIs and Richard rose from their holes, stared at each other, confused. They brushed dirt off their overcoats and looked at their guns caked with snow. A German patrol could walk in and knock them all out.

"We're sitting ducks," Groaner said.

The Sergeant set up the defensive positions and Richard was assigned to stand guard at Outpost Two. He went up to the dilapidated log cabin, part of the old German defensive network and relieved Watson and Henderson, two GIs from Pittsburgh, who were were inseparable, cheery fellows, always laughing at Pennsylvania Dutch jokes and sharing everything – even guard duty. Richard could hardly tell them apart except that Watson had long thick sideburns and Henderson close-cropped hair.

"How's everything?" Richard asked.

"It's a picnic," Henderson said.

"We're in a boring holding action," Watson said. "Nothing to it. We did see a yellow flare that lit up Stein. It's down there, all right."

"I'd sure like to get me a German before the war ends," Henderson said.

"I won't cry if I never run into a German," Watson said.

"I'll take over," Richard said. "Did you see anybody when the flare went up?"

"No," Henderson said. "I don't believe there are any Germans a hundred yards from us."

The two left and Richard stood guard outside the door of the old wooden cabin. The snow came down hard, turning into a minor blizzard. He shook from the cold despite his overcoat, field jacket and long unwieldy scarf and felt a sudden painful throbbing in his left foot, which he figured was frostbite.

It was late afternoon, yet the snow made everything dark and hazy like evening coming on. The evergreens made him think of the woods below his house. Smiley had reminded them it was Christmas and he thought of how the snow outside their farm made strings of lace on the mountain firs.

He tried to envision Stein in the valley. Was the town really such a threat to them or just a figment of the imagination of frightened officers? The snow whirled about him, blown by the breath of an unseen power. Were the enemy soldiers real or imaginary inhabitants of a ghost town? If enemy scouts were guarding the town on the outskirts, dressed as GIs, how could he protect his own men in the holes behind him if he couldn't see anybody? If there were German divisions in the valley, thousands of their soldiers could be hiding in the trees and in the ditches carved in the snow. He stared into the foggy woods, trying to identify any outline of a soldier but it was like staring at a huge white sheet stretched from tree to tree. If he went into that whiteness he would be lost. If he moved back toward the sleeping men he'd lose contact with any sudden intruder who came through the white sheet. And what if a German circumvented the cabin and came at him from behind?

Well, he thought, it must be normal at the front for everything to be fouled up, but he figured things would turn out alright, if he was careful.

To cheer himself up he tore out a page from his poetry book and with the stub of a pencil he carried, he began writing his letter. Timmons came by to join him in the cabin.

"What are you writing?" he asked.

"I'm writing a letter to Gloria. She'll be amazed by what we're going through."

"You're wasting your time, buddy. She didn't come to see you off from town. She hasn't written you more than a note. Give her up, friend."

"I can't. I'm sure when I get back she'll be as lovely as ever."

"She works in the fields under the hot sun. She'll be a wrinkled old cow when you come back."

"Don't be such a jerk, Timmons. And when Gloria finds out what we've done she'll be proud of us."

"Well, dream on, my friend."

Richard finished his letter:

> *Dear Gloria,*
>
> *This must be a short note. I'm sitting here in a cabin, on guard duty. Luckily our Captain knows what we're going to do, so we*

*are confident everything will work out alright.
I'm with my friend, Timmons. I buck him up
when he's depressed. But I tell him–we're ready
for our first real test.*

*I have a story to tell you. We ran into
Joe DiMaggio here at the front. He was peeling
potatoes, working for the USO. Timmons asked
him to show us his swing and Joe swung for us,
with the photographer taking his picture.*

*Two things keep me going – the need to
destroy this madman Hitler, and my memory of
you. Sounds corny, but, Gloria, I think of you all
the time. And I kiss your photo you sent me.*

*Hope you don't mind my signing this
letter –*

Love,
Richard
*P.S. I enclose a poem I'm writing about
our arrival at the front.*

Arriving at the Front

Richard could hardly believe
he'd come to the front
with enemy soldiers
down in the valley
a hundred yards away.
He'd read a story once
about a Russian boy
who thought the front
a magical place
where death would stalk him
in the killing woods.

Now trapped in the rising fog
he couldn't tell
a friend from a foe –
the snow that suddenly
came falling hard
was like a paperweight
which, turned around,
would make the flakes
inside the glass
come swirling down.

An orange flare shot up
above the firs
as in a dream.
His company had moved
into an abstract
unseen landscape
far from the lucid photos
of the enemy country
taken in the sun.

Arriving at the woods
he breathed a sigh of relief
for they had passed
the first test
in their accommodation with the war –
which stationed them
in a zone of terror
where they could hear
a liberating cry
on the field of death.

Timmons had wandered off into the fog, to find out when the next food would be dished out. Richard, having addressed his letter, sat down at the edge of the door. It was getting dark. He hadn't slept much in the bivouac area when they arrived. He took guard seriously but he was new to the front and for a second lost concentration – set his head against the side of the cabin door and, thinking of Gloria, soon fell asleep.

2

When he was eighteen three things altered Richard's life. He became obsessed by love poetry, he resolved to join the army, and he met Gloria.

He kept on the shelf above his bed the book with the poems of Marlowe and Donne he loved. He would memorize his favorites and walk about the garden reciting the lines that captivated him.

> Come live with me and be my love,
> And we will all the pleasures prove
>
> I wonder by my troth, what thou and I
> Did till we loved?

His mother, looking out the window, smiled as she watched him reciting his lines. She was proud of him – she too had loved poetry and when Richard was very young she read to him the lyrics of Edward Lear and Lewis Carroll.

In his college course in French literature he read *The Life of Eleanor of Aquitaine* and was fascinated by the troubadours who wrote songs about their beautiful women. In the class he also read the story of Lancelot, who went through ghastly trials to rescue Guinevere from a monster.

Richard dreamt that someday he too might be tested – perhaps in the coming war – and a beautiful girl would fall in love with him. He never mentioned this to his fellow students, who would say he was obsessed by such romantic bunk.

At the time he was shocked by the news that Adolf Hitler had ordered the burning of Jewish women and children in ovens, and he resolved to leave college, join the army to fight *this* monster. His father, a veteran of World War I, approved of his decision.

Then one afternoon at a local Spring Harvest Dance in the

auditorium of a country school in Allentown he met Gloria. He'd taken a seat beside her on a bench and was attracted by her round, doll-like face, with a smattering of freckles on her cheeks, a mole on one side of her lip, lovely blonde hair, with a red rose in her barrette, and a sturdy body like a Gauguin maid with heavy breasts. She wore a tight-fitting skirt with a black leather jacket, high boots, with long dangling earrings like world globes, and jangling bracelets on each arm.

He thought she was the most beautiful woman he'd ever seen.

He turned to her and asked, "Can I buy you a drink?"

She looked him over and said, "Why not?"

"I'm Richard."

"I'm Gloria," and she laughed, for no particular reason he could discern.

A pretty waitress came up to them, dressed in short pants like a cheerleader and in an embarrassingly tight blouse revealing her breasts. She looked down at her costume, smiling to let them know she thought her required garb was stupid. Gloria nodded to the woman that she understood, then ordered two large cokes.

Three musicians came in and began to assemble their equipment on the small bandstand – a pianist, a clarinet player and a drummer.

When the drinks came Gloria took out a small bottle of rum from her purse and added quite a bit to their paper cups. "I really need a pick-me-up," she said.

The strong drink made Richard feel free as the wind, his face flushed. And he saw that Gloria had an off-key smile, signifying she was slightly roused by the rum. He was pleased because he could only dance with her – as he was planning to do – if they both had enough rum.

She chugalugged her drink, then said, "You know why I drink? When I'm sober, I feel I've nothing in my head."

"I drink," he said, "to find out where I'm going. And right now I'm drinking to find out where I'm going with you."

She laughed and he reached to take her hand but she withdrew it.

They ordered another round of cokes from the waitress and realizing they were good customers she brought a free plate of small sausages with little buns. Gloria picked out a sausage while Richard took two and wrapped them in a bun. Then she poured the rum again into their cups.

The band began to play *I Can't Give you Anything But Love* and Richard and Gloria moved to the dance floor, where there was only one other couple.

He was amazed how easily she followed him, twisting in response to his moves, her face red with pleasure. He thought how wonderful it was, as the author Sterne said, when the spirit mixes with the dance.

When they returned to their table for a break she said, "You really let yourself go."

He tried once more to take her hand but she smiled and withdrew it again.

"Let's get out of here," she said. "I want to show you something."

He paid the bill, tipped the pleasant waitress and they left the auditorium and walked down to the lake which edged the school grounds.

A freight came through the narrow passage just north of the lake, dragging its endless cars like a scene from a surreal movie. Perhaps it was the rum drink but Richard thought it odd the way the train engine hooted like an endangered species, shattering the quiet air, disappearing like a wiggling dragon into the tunnel's cavernous hole below the hill.

Gloria took him to a long winding staircase that dropped down to a small sandy cove by the lake. Her face was flushed from the drink and also, he figured, from her awareness that she was leading him on.

"I want to show you Dido's Cave," she said, drawing him to a small rock cave at the lake's edge beneath the cliffs. Laughing, she drew him inside, where they sat on the sand –

and saw the tunnel leading out to the water like it was at the long end of binoculars.

"What are you thinking about?" she asked.

"Well, I was thinking about a poem I'd like you to hear."

"If you insist."

He said,

> There is a garden in her face,
> Where roses and white lilies grow,
> A heavenly paradise is that place,
> Wherein all pleasant fruits do flow.

"Isn't that the most beautiful poem you've ever heard?"

Gloria gave out a cackling sound and he wondered what was happening. She couldn't restrain herself but began to giggle and then exploded with a loud laugh until she couldn't stop.

"What's so funny?" he said, trying to smile.

When her spasm of laughter subsided she said, "I was imagining a garden in her face. I can see weeds sprouting in her cheeks." She went on laughing and he finally joined in, but she could tell he was upset.

"Don't mind me," she said. "I'm in a silly mood. Blame it on the rum." But she continued to laugh, then said, "I know a poem one of the farm girls told me –

> There was a young lover named Kildare
> Who had sex with a girl on the stair.
> The banister broke
> But he doubled his stroke
> And finished her off in mid-air.

She roared with laughter and Richard smiled, though he was still subdued by her reaction to his favorite poem, but he said, "That's a good limerick."

When she calmed down she said, "Richard, tell me. Have

you ever really *had* a girl?"

"I knew a girl, Miranda, in high school. I used to walk her home. She was a tall willowy girl. We had some fun in the woods but she would always stop short of the real thing."

"So you're a free man and you're looking for a new flame?"

Again he tried to take her hand but she held back, saying, "I'm glad you're unsure of yourself like me. Rollo thinks he knows everything. Sometimes I think I might just have to wash him out of my hair, as the song goes. Richard, you seem to understand things. That's why you can be a good friend. You're not condescending. You listen to me, as silly as I am."

He leaned over and managed to plant a kiss on her cheek but she suddenly stood up. "I hate to leave you so unsatisfied," she said, "but I really have to settle this thing with Rollo. And you and I will probably never really be lovers, will we?"

As she left in her own car Richard was still captivated by her, muttering, "What a beautiful girl."

A few nights later he ran into his friend Timmons at the local bar. After a few beers he said, "Timmy, I've met the most marvelous girl."

"What's her name?" his friend said.

"Gloria Heckewelder."

"Hecky? I know her. I worked on a farm with her one summer."

"Isn't she a knockout?"

"I wouldn't say that. She has glorious tits, a wonderful ass. But she's slightly cross-eyed. And she has that mole on her lips, with hairs sticking out like a mustache. And she's a tough cookie. But I love Pennsylvania Dutch girls like Gloria, with straw in their teeth, who sing a dirty song while they work. And when you hump them they moo like a cow. I had a ball with Gloria's friend, Jolly."

"I wish you wouldn't talk about Gloria like that."

"Let me tell you. When we were picking apples together, she stank to high heaven. She never took a bath."

"I think you're talking about somebody else. When I danced with her she had a lovely odor, a special violet perfume."

"Okay. But let me tell you something else," he said, laughing. "She could curse in that husky mannish voice of hers. If somebody cut in front of her when she wanted to climb a tree for apples, she'd shout, 'Gott-damn Bull's sickle' – God damn bull's prick. I'd never heard a girl swear like that in my life. Her voice could crack a bell at a hundred yards."

"I don't want to hear any more. And stop spreading gossip about Gloria. She's respectable and comes from a good family – her father's superintendent in the blast furnace at Bethlehem Steel and that's not a mean job."

"Well, tell me. Did you screw her?"

"No. And I don't think you have to screw every woman you meet. Right now I can only think how beautiful she is."

"Well, I wish you luck. But women know if you know how to do it. And if they find out you don't know how, they'll turn you down because they think you'll get them pregnant. But they get as horny as we do and if they see you know what you're doing, they'll give in every time."

That night Richard wondered why Gloria wouldn't kiss him. Could Timmons be right – he was too innocent to appeal to girls? And though one or two seemed to be aroused by his kisses, they let him know he wasn't going the whole way.

But he was sure Gloria would come around once she got to know him. And once he joined the army and went overseas to fight against Hitler's army, surely she'd be his girl.

God, he thought, as he got into bed, how beautiful she was.

3

In a dream Richard heard what sounded like a cat whining and he was running out of the house, his mother trying to hold him back. He had to stumble over the piled snow behind the farm, following the cry down to the cliffs, where he crawled through a huge water pipe the way he had done as a kid playing war. He came out on the ghetto side of town. A woman in a black dress with a dog barking at her heels moved in and out of a line of clothes blackened by the mill smoke. He looked out over the canal, where they'd gone swimming on summer days, wading into the "nigger shit" as the ghetto kids called the murky water – climbing on to old tires and paddling out to an island between the stinking canal and the dying river.

An empty boat drifted in the canal, the oil bubbling up from the tragedy where a steel worker had drowned. In the dream he felt he could've saved the man if his mother hadn't held him back that extra second and he cursed himself as a slow Samaritan.

Waking in the early morning light he heard the high whine that had triggered the dream. He realized he had fallen asleep on guard, endangering the others. The whining or sobbing went on, now out of control.

A foot seemed to brush against some branches below the cabin. He pushed his gun's safety catch forward, his heart thumping. The wind didn't let up and the pelting snow soaked his face and gun. A sudden flare shot up above the firs, giving the trees a cotton-textured glow, in which a shadowy figure appeared as if hiding behind a yellow gauze screen. The light flickered in an arc and died. Richard whispered to the hidden figure, "Horsefeathers," waiting for the password, "Harpo." "Horsefeathers," he said again, making a sighing sound a German might think was the wind.

He lay down on his stomach just outside the cabin, his gun ready, finger on the trigger. When a German came through the woods, they said, it sounded like a herd of elephants. But what he heard was hardly audible and he began sweating. "Horsefeathers," he said softly. But there was no answer. He looked at the rising mist, imagining a quiet ghost sliding through. He steadied his gun and got the figure in his sights. Could it be somebody from his own company? The figure moved out of his line of vision but Richard kept his gun aimed at the spot, hoping for another sighting of the intruder, when an arm was thrown around his neck and he was straining to turn his head in the vise.

"It's me," Timmons said, releasing the pressure on his friend's neck.

"Why didn't you give the password?"

"I didn't hear you. I thought you were a German."

"What's going on?"

Timmons pointed to a slice of valley where the fog had blown away. "I've done some scouting down there. I got a couple of yards from the road into Stein and I saw some spooky figures moving around."

"Did you hear somebody whining, like a cat?"

"That was the Captain. He's actually crying. He's pure jelly – he can't budge from his hole. He's loaded down with grenades. I asked him what was wrong. He said, 'There are booby traps everywhere. If I move, I'll be blown skyhigh.' Remember in Basic he was always fascinated by booby traps. Now he can't stand the thought of real ones."

He took a small bottle from his coat pocket. "Want some Calvados? Some GI must've abandoned it."

Richard drank from the bottle and got a burning in his throat that made him cough. Then a warm rush went through his body. "I hope it's good for my foot," he said. "The medic told me to stay off my feet."

"Rub it every night with spit. And keep moving! I don't get frostbite like the others because I don't stay in one place too long. Those poor scared bunnies like Groaner – they're afraid to stick their heads out of a hole. I can't sleep – I've been wandering around. I know these woods like a woman's butt."

He took a drink from the bottle.

In the distance a truck came out of a draw and moved down the road; another followed, then another, their motors humming. Several cars raced their motors and they heard the sounds as if from a loudspeaker. The acoustics of the snow-covered valley were perfect. Four tanks oozed out of the same draw, the men beside them bunched together in columns. Some were turning flashlights on and off, making arcs above the road. A snaking line appeared – of artillery guns, trucks, tanks and men.

"That's what I saw before," Timmons said.

"Why are they making such a hullabaloo?" Richard asked.

"I don't know."

A muffled song came from the marchers below. "They're singing, for God's sake," Timmons said. "Why don't we fire our big guns at them?

"They wanted to fire but their ammunition never came up."

"The Germans aren't crazy, are they?"

"No. Maybe they want us to think they're going south. Maybe they're playing games and they're not going south at all. They know we're looking down on them too. They built this cabin."

"Yeah, and the Colonel never changed our positions from the original enemy defenses. The Germans have us all zeroed in; they can hit us any time they want to, right in the old bread basket."

A brilliant white flare shot up like a Fourth of July rocket, turning the morning, now that the fog had blown away, into a bright noon. Searchlights flickered on and off.

"Don't budge," Richard said.

Another flare lit up the cabin, putting them in the limelight and a shell came screaming over their heads. They felt naked and exposed.

There were cries behind them, someone hollering, "Medic!" and Richard raced toward the camp in the blazing light, with Timmons following in a rush to get to the protective mist. They

25

came to a secluded wood area and stopped in front of three figures.

"It looks like a patrol," Timmons said.

Three men were kneeling forward in the snow as if waiting for a breathing space in the firing in order to edge ahead. But they were frozen in a tableau of readiness, like a training photo showing how to creep and crawl. Richard checked the nearest who was doubled up on his side as if from a stomach ache. Turning him slightly he found a jagged shell hole in his coat. He could find no pulse. The second GI, his helmet beside him, was sunk deep in the snow, his hair a clotted dark red mass. His blood had drawn red wiggly lines on the sheet of snow. The last man in the patrol had been struck in the head.

"One shell must've done it for all three," Richard said. "We can't do anything for them."

"Who are they?" Timmons asked.

"I think I recognize the first guy – Martin from K Company."

"We can't just sit here and let them have target practice on us."

The blood on the snow was fresh. These guys, Richard thought, had been walking through the woods like himself seconds before. Now they were non-persons, their blood spilled out in ugly streaks. The whirlwind of the blow had made the last one in the tableau a grotesque model of a man. Had they accomplished anything before the sky fell on them? Did they ever think they might go so quickly to that *other side of night* – as one of the poets called death.

There was no action at all, but Richard had a few sleepless nights, thinking about their precarious position. One morning the Captain picked out a lead squad – the Sergeant, Richard and Timmons. They all were aware of the anxiety in the officer's face which was powdered with talcum, his long blonde hair sticking out of his helmet. He still had his gas mask and grenade pouch, which the others, except for Timmons, had tossed away as useless baggage. A walking ammo dump, a GI called the officer.

The GIs despised the Captain – he had bragged too much about his women. In a village on their way to the front he had been given a bath by a French woman – the least she could do for him, he said, for saving her country. He was getting ready for "further business," as he put it, when a shell careened into the back of her house with a blast like a demolition ball. Half of her cottage was blown away. She was running around screaming and he had to dress, his "business unfulfilled." The account got little sympathy from the men, who had no chance to meet local women.

The Captain gave each of them a sheet with a hole in it, telling them to poke twigs all around their helmet liners, so they'd look like a white mound with a bush on top.

"Stay ten feet apart," he told them. "After me, the Sergeant, Richard and Timmons. We're the eyes of the regiment. If you see anything move, freeze. If you draw fire hit the ground and creep and crawl like an Indian."

They walked alongside a row of firs and came to the top of a curving cleft that dropped down a hillside, a deep gash in the snowy slope of the mountain that was easy to climb down, but which was visible to enemy artillery. Timmons went up to the officer.

"Captain," he said, "we don't go this way – it's Purple Heart Alley. The Germans have this area all zeroed in. You go that way and you'll get sprayed all over the branches."

"We go straight down," the Captain said. "It's the quickest way."

"Begging your pardon, Sir, it's the quickest way to a grave," Timmons said. "We don't go that way. I've done some reconnoitering while you all were back there in the camp playing with yourselves. I know a path that will ease us down toward Stein without being seen."

"Shut up, Timmons," the Sergeant said. "We follow the Captain."

They moved off down the path, crossed over a snowy ridge; lifting their arms, they waved their sheets like a Halloween troop.

Timmons stepped gingerly in the snow, imagining a German behind every tree. It was dumb to risk his neck for a jerk off Captain. Suddenly there were cracking sounds as bullets struck the trees on either side of them.

"We've established contact," the Captain said, his whisper wavering in the cold.

"How do you know who was firing at us?" Timmons asked.

A mortar shell came screaming over and they all hit the snow. They heard a swishing sound and a shell exploded not far from them. Richard thought of the artillery guns fired on maneuvers, muffled and far off. These guns were firing real shells.

"Come on, let's get out of here," Timmons said. "We can't hang around this alley."

They pushed through the screen of trees and on a hill across from them Richard made out a row of men in white like themselves, moving as if in a dream, like a white river.

But it wasn't a dream. The soldiers, so unreal in his imagination, must be flesh-and-blood Germans across from him, in white camouflage, reflections in a mirror of their own white shapes.

One of the figures raised a gun and pointing it in their direction fired at them. Richard laid his gun on the edge of the ditch and, aiming at the threatening soldier, squeezed the trigger, feeling a shock of pain as the gun slammed back into his lip.

"What are you shooting at?" the Captain asked.

"I saw something move near those trees," Richard said, pointing across.

"Did it have a bushy tail?" the Sergeant said.

"Look," Richard said, "About a hundred yards left of that

road."

"Don't fire," the Captain said, lying low in a ditch, "you're asking for trouble."

A whistling sound cut the air and the branches crackled as bullets hit the trees. Richard put his gun on the edge and fired away, raking the trees where he saw a line of white shapes getting set to fire on them. Timmons stretched out in the ditch and fired across the road. Richard looked over, saw a helmet, then a shoulder; he fired and hit one of the tree limbs, shaking the snow loose. He was sweating, even in the cold.

He thought of the boy in Stephen Crane's story of the Civil War, waiting for his first battle – how the enemy soldiers came screaming down the hill toward him and in sudden terror he threw down his gun and ran. He figured he wouldn't run. What scared him was that he might be mutilated. They had sulpha for all wounds, but he thought of all the places a bullet or shell could strike him – in the eyes or groin. The awesome German units were rumored to be in the vicinity. A steel helmet was all he had to ward off a blow. With the best camouflage in the world, a shell could drop on him out of the blue. He could be blinded or castrated.

He was thirsty and took a quick drink from his canteen. Timmons was firing away and, in between shots, sucked on a chocolate bar like a monkey. The snow came down, drenching their coats and guns. Richard dried his M-1 with his handkerchief, wondering if he could hit anybody in the driving snow.

The forces on the opposite ridge returned their fire with a rap-rap beat. Richard and Timmons continued to fire until their clips were empty. Then there was an odd silence. They looked up and saw two soldiers come out of the woods across from them, their hands raised up, one of them waving a white handkerchief.

As they approached, Richard recognized Watson and Henderson.

"What were you guys doing?" the Sergeant asked.

"We got separated," Watson said. "We thought you were Germans."

"We beat you, fair and square," Timmons said, laughing.

"Screw you," Henderson said.

A shell shattered the air overhead, making them all flatten out.

"See what you guys have done," the Captain said. "You stirred up a hornet's nest."

Groaner wandered over to join them and the Captain said, "Get down."

"I can't," he said.

"Christ, Groaner, it's only your first shelling," the Sergeant said. "Get your ass into the trench."

The sky glowed with the reflection of a fire. A cloud of red smoke poured up from the distant pines. Another shell crashed and exploded next to the spot where Timmons was crunched down, splattering snow on his head.

"Let's get out of here," the Captain said. "Follow me."

He was off and running, some men behind him racing through the world of level, unending snow. Suddenly he was swallowed up in a hole and Timmons crawled forward, looking down into the deep pit where the officer was flailing about in the melting snow.

"Follow me," Timmons said, mocking the Captain as he helped the officer climb up to the edge of the trench – a sump of frozen garbage packed at the bottom.

"Groaner, get down," Richard yelled from his end of the ditch.

"No," the man said, lying paralyzed in the open. It was quiet, and yet Groaner's panic prevailed. He was curled up in the snow, moaning, "If I move, they'll fire again."

A blast from the valley below punctuated his words and a shell exploded behind them. Machine gun fire kicked up snow on all sides.

"See, I told you," Groaner said, his shoulders hunched over, cowed, his head shaking.

"Groaner," the Sergeant said, "it's your imagination. Get down here with us."

"I'm not getting into my grave," Groaner said.

"How did we ever get such a jellyfish?" Timmons said.

Another round of machine gun fire sprayed the area and they heard a sound like a hand drawn across a piano wire and Groaner was screaming. The Sergeant went to him and found his mouth wide open, his jaw stripped down, his teeth bleeding, with shreds of flesh hanging down like thin wisps of a beard. He was wriggling in the snow like he was practicing a swimming stroke, rocking from side to side as if to increase his speed against the pull of the water. With a yell he shook as if to free himself from the snow that was drowning him, soaking up his blood like a sponge. Then suddenly resigning himself to the undercurrent he stretched out like he wanted to sleep. The Sergeant checked him, ran his hand under his coat and felt the wounds, drawing his hands out bloodied, his fist clutching the banjo and frayed, intestine-like strings, which the shells had struck.

The lanky Tennessean had been a sentimental slob but as a casualty replacement he'd become one of the Company. Only Timmons refused to give him any sympathy. "The guy was a jerk," he said. "He wouldn't even crawl into the ditch."

"I told you guys a hundred times," the Sergeant said, "you got to take cover."

Rabbit and Rule came up, the latter shouldering a bazooka he had appropriated. "What's happening?" Rabbit asked.

"Groaner's dead," the Captain said. "It was his own fault."

"He shit a brick," Timmons said, grimacing and nodding at Groaner.

The Captain turned on them. "You guys better get used to a corpse grinning at you."

The shelling of their position picked up again, continuing for what seemed like hours. Machine gun fire crackled in a sporadic chitchat of enemy fire. Snow whirled about like crystals on a holiday crèche.

31

Later when it was quiet Richard went behind some firs to piss, and coming back got separated from the others. He couldn't locate the Sergeant or anyone else. A rifleman passed by, stumbling ahead of whizzing bullets, holding up his arm that hung at an odd angle in its gauze wrapping.

"The Germans are everywhere," he said.

Richard wondered how they could be coming in on all sides when there hadn't been any personal contact with the enemy. Was his outfit being blown back in a shameful way? Another GI came by, his arm about a friend for support, a white bandage circling his thigh. They walked by without speaking, as if their wounds told their story.

Flares suddenly climbed the skies, coloring the clear air with grey, red, green and amber lights. After the spears of light hit the ground the GI and his buddy moved off.

A shell sailed over Richard and landed close, the blast rustling his OD pants. Another shell came over and he gritted his teeth and admonished the incoming shell, "No, no, no." Then it was quiet again.

As they settled down in their trenches later, Timmons said, "What a fuck-up. And we end up shooting at our own guys."

"It's the snow," Richard said. "We can't see anybody. But you wondered if you could shoot at someone. Well, you did. It just so happened – you fired at our own troops."

The next afternoon Richard, Timmons and the Captain were walking into an unreal landscape, far from the lucid photos of the enemy country taken in the sun. Walking carefully across a hill of snow, afraid of mines, Richard wondered if a hand might reach out of the snow and tear him apart.

They came to a cabin abandoned by the Germans. And once inside Richard found in a desk drawer the photo of a soldier, tall and lean, in a Sergeant's uniform, embracing a short blond boy. Startled, he saw it was Karl from the college who had once said he didn't want to go home to serve in the war.

A few days later they came upon an enemy outpost in the woods where Timmons looked through a hedge and saw two German soldiers resting from combat. Timmons, pointing out the soldiers on the other side of the hedge, asked the Captain what they should do and the officer said he should toss a grenade through the trees and Richard should do the same. The two then threw their grenades which exploded and, soon after, they went cautiously into the clearing and saw the bodies of two young men who must've been eating sandwiches, their guns lying unattended by their sides. A beefy soldier, his face puffed out balloon-like, was doubled up with a red hole beneath his belt. The other young man was cut in two, each half in a pool of blood. Turning the body over, Richard saw a face which seemed frozen in a boyish grin – his friend Karl's face.

During an afternoon lull the next day Richard sat down in a ditch, took out a page from his book and wrote to his family:

> *Dear mother and dad,*
>
> *It's hard to write at this moment. But I'm okay.*
>
> *I miss you all very much. I guess some of your letters have never reached me, for the communications are poor because we're in a war zone.*
>
> *I just hope the Red Cross courier gets my letters out.*
>
> *It's very cold here in the Ardennes woods. But my huge woolen coat keeps me warm. It's amusing to get into a chow line in the blinding snow and hardly know what food they're splashing on my mess plate. Yet here at*

the front we get roast beef, potatoes, beans, ice cream and cake.

I'm still with Timmons, who can be vulgar at times but he reminds me of my days at home.

Can you believe it – I went into an enemy cabin and found a photo of my college friend, Karl, a soldier in the German army?

We've had our first taste of action. But, Dad, you'll understand why I can't tell you much about our maneuvers, for security reasons. We still have Captain Plankton to lead us. And the German artillery is so ineffectual we've had few casualties.

Mother, thanks for the book, "The Power of Positive Thinking." I'll look forward to reading it.

Say hello to my friends.

Love,

Richard

P.S. I enclose a poem I just started about my friend Karl.

You'll say I'm making this up
but stationed in a cabin
abandoned by the Germans
I found a photo of a soldier
tall and lean, in a Sergeant's garb
embracing a short blonde boy.

Startled I saw it was Karl from school
who told me once he didn't relish
going home to serve in the war –
who, taking my hand as we drank,
had talked in somber tones
of poetry and winter sports.

And here I was, marching across
the Snow Mountain, to ferret out
my friend among the frozen pines,
standing like snow-clad skeletons,
and kill him – who once had talked
of sacred love in the Grecian isles.

Before he fell asleep that night Richard wondered how long
he had been at the front. Despite the noisy guns in the distance,
exhaustion took over and he cradled himself in a cold dark
hole.

He dreamt he was on a beach at home with Gloria. She took
off her straw hat and let her long blonde hair fall about her
shoulders. Cradling his head on her stomach she caressed his
cheek and he ran his fingers around her neck as if they were
horses wanting to run free between her breasts. She pushed him
away, put on her bathing cap and ran for a swim. He dashed
after her into the shallows, catching her in the water, where he
pulled her down. She threw her head back and he squeezed her
and she laughed and wriggled like a fish that had just been
caught.

Waking, he was delighted by the dream. And it was some
time before he thought about the danger from the shells and
tried again to make sense of what was happening.

4

Dispirited by the confusion at the front, Richard and Timmons often remembered how they had been tricked at the local Induction Center into serving their country – which still left a bitter taste in their mouths, though Richard tried to excuse the Army's unfair treatment of them.

At the time Richard, driven by his hatred for Adolf Hitler, had left college to enlist in the service and soon went to the Induction Center along with his friend Timmons.

In the large high school gym, crowded with young nervous inductees, Richard and Timmons stood before Captain Plankton, who would follow them through most of their service days – a tall officer, mustached, his blonde hair slicked back with grease, a nose that was too long – almost handsome, like the character in the old movies who doesn't get the girl. He wore especially tailored OD's, a beret tilted at a jaunty angle and wore all the ribbons a Captain could wear who hadn't yet been oversees or in combat.

Now he looked down from his desk chair on Richard and Timmons in their low chairs, his lip turned up as if he were scowling at them.

"So you guys want to sign up?" he said.

"Yes," Richard said.

"That's great. Well, you're lucky – you came at the right time."

"How's that?" Timmons asked.

"Well, there's a great offer that just came down from Washington. If you sign up now, you don't have to take a physical. You'll have your pick of any service. And you'll have the opportunity to become an officer. You probably will remain in the States until the war's over."

"Sounds good," Timmons said.

"I'd like to sign up for Artillery," Richard said. "I was trained for that in my college ROTC."

"Artillery? You got it. And your friend?"

"I'll take Artillery too."

"Why not," the Captain said, smiling; "Just sign the forms."

They signed the papers and the officer said, "We need fellows like you."

And within a week they received their orders to report to an Infantry outfit in Macon, Georgia as buck privates.

In the train going south Timmons said, "Richard, the Captain screwed us royally."

"I guess they need bodies now."

"Don't excuse him. He said we'd get Artillery but sent us to the Infantry."

"Maybe he had no choice."

"Don't defend the creep. And I bet we don't get Officer's Training either."

"I'm willing to serve in the Infantry. It's where the action is. My father and Gloria – they'll be proud of me."

When they settled in the barracks at Fort Macon they found out that Captain Plankton had come south too and was now in charge of their company. On the morning after their arrival he made an announcement from his office microphone, which was broadcast to every floor in the barracks, "Will Private Richard Glasgow and Private Timmons Clark get their asses down here to my office on the double."

They stopped making their beds and rushed down to the office where the Captain was leaning back in his swivel chair, a full glass in his hand, a bottle of Jack Daniels open on the table.

"Okay, give me a salute," he said.

They saluted him and he casually returned the gesture.

"Now listen, you flunkies. You're in the army and you obey all orders, right?"

"Yes, Sir," Richard said.

"Captain," Timmons said, "you told us we'd be sent to the

Artillery."

"That's tough shit. Now I have a job for both of you. Look out the window. Do you see about a hundred yards from here that dog turd on the training ground?"

"I don't see anything," Timmons said.

"Well, you two privates run over there and pick up that turd and bring it back and deposit it in the trash can in front of the barracks."

Richard walked out, followed by Timmons who was shaking his head in anger. When they got to the training field Richard pretended to pick something up and wrap it in a fragment of trash paper. They came back and Richard deposited his paper in the trash can while the Captain roared with laughter in his office.

Back in their quarters, Timmons said, "I'd like to kick his butt."

"I'm glad you didn't," Richard said.

"That asshole had no right to make us do something so stupid."

"Maybe he wants to see if we'll obey orders, however absurd."

"That's bullshit."

"If you kicked him you'd end up in the stockade."

"I don't care. I would've felt better."

"Timmons, you're beginning to sound like all the rest of them, always bitching. These guys get better chow than they've ever had in their lives back in Hicksville – steak, French fries, freshly made bread, ice cream. And they say – what shit. They bitch about the weather, which is all they can talk about. And watch them bitch when they get to the front."

"Well, they have a right to bitch."

During the training period Timmons was a constant thorn in the Captain's side. In the wooded area, where the company was

38

protected from the hot Georgia sun, the officer showed the assembled soldiers how to pull the pin from a grenade. Timmons raised his hand.

"Is this an important question, Timmons?" the Captain asked, upset at being interrupted.

"Oh yes, Captain. I think you got it wrong. I've seen this in the movies. You pull the pin out with your teeth."

"Yes, dummy. And you'd have no teeth left."

During the lecture on VD at the company theater, with films showing the deterioration of the male organ from clap or syphilis, Timmons raised his hand.

"Is it one of your stupid questions, Timmons?" the Captain said.

"Oh no, sir."

"Well make it quick."

"You've kept us out on bivouac for two weeks. You haven't given us any weekend passes, right?"

"That's because this division of nincompoops has the highest VD rate in the U.S."

"Well, if you confine us to the area and we can't go to town, how are we going to get the clap?"

The others laughed and one said, "Right on, Timmons."

"Don't be a wise-ass," the Captain said, resigned.

One night Richard and Timmons went to a dance at the USO headquarters in Macon, and there they saw colorful balloons hanging from the ceiling of the huge hall, for Halloween Night. Carved pumpkins grinned from the corners. A few dance hostesses at the tables wore macabre masks and nondescript costumes. One woman wore the sluttish dress of a prostitute; another was made up as a pregnant nun in a black, full-blown habit and dark veil.

While waiting for entertainment, Richard went to a phone booth in a corner of the hall and, inserting more quarters than required, dialed Gloria's number.

"Hello," she said.

"Hi, Gloria."

"Who's this?"

"It's Richard."

"Oh, hi. What's up?"

"I'm in the army."

"How is it?"

"Okay. I'm with my friend, Timmons. How are you?"

"I've got a very bad cold."

"I'm sorry to hear that."

"To hear what?"

"That you've got a cold."

"You say you're with a guy named Timmons. Could that be Timmons Clark?"

"Yes, why do you ask?"

"I worked in the fields with him. He's a great guy. Of course, he's not into books like you."

"I know. By the way, Gloria, would you send me your picture?"

"I guess I can. Oh, Richard, Dad's got an important call coming. Could you buzz me another time?"

"Sure. But it's great to hear your voice."

"Nice to talk to you."

And he hung up.

He called home, collect, and his father accepted the call.

"Hi, dad," he said.

"Well, Richard, it's great to hear from you. How's the soldier?"

"Everything's fine. I'm here with Timmons."

"I hope you ditch that fellow – he's not up to your caliber."

"Oh he's a good pal. And Captain Plankton is in charge of the company. He signed us up at the Induction Center and was transferred here to Macon, Georgia."

"I know Plankton. I played golf with him. A solid chap. He used to be in charge of the University ROTC here at Lehigh.

Give him my regards."

"He didn't give us Artillery. We're assigned to the Infantry."

"He probably got his orders from higher-up. I expect you'll become officers. I wrote my friend General Briggs in Washington. He used to work with me at the Steel Company when I became Treasurer. He wrote back that he'll use his influence to have you sent to Officers' Training. He's excited about a friend of his – General Eisenhower, the Supreme Commander of the Allied forces. Briggs says he's a brilliant tactician who planned the invasion of Europe. With his leadership, Richard, the war should be over quickly, and you can come home. Now say a word to your mother."

"Hello, mother."

"Hello, dear. I've been listening on the other phone. It's good to hear your voice. I'm missing you already."

"I miss you too."

"Are you eating well?"

"The food's fine."

"You're keeping warm at night?"

"Yes."

"Do you get enough sleep?"

"Yes, until one of the guys snores."

"I'm sorry you're in the Infantry but I'm glad you're with our friend Captain Plankton. You must write often."

"I'll write."

"What?"

"I think we have a bad connection," his father said. "Can you call us another time?"

"Good night, Dickie," his mother said. "We'll be thinking about you."

Richard hung up and went to a table at the side of the hall to write a letter to Gloria.

A woman who'd arrived at the dance hall had attracted

41

Timmons – her face painted in dark, curving lines, her lashes a thick black, her face smudged with heavy white powder. A wreath of golden marigolds hung from her neck over a long grey dress – her skin showing through the embroidery. He thought she looked like the cadaverous figure sold at the souvenir shops.

He noticed a glazed look in her eyes, as if she were having trouble focusing and he hoped she wasn't on drugs. She might be in her late thirties or early forties, he figured – the makeup hardly masking any age lines.

She came up and with her skeletal face seemed like an apparition to him.

"That's a great Halloween costume," he said.

"It's not for Halloween," she said. "It's a dress for the *Dia de los Muertos*, the day of the dead. Marigolds are the flowers for the departed. Now's our chance to dance for the dead. Come on, let's show them." She tossed her black boots under the table.

The band began playing, and taking him by the hand she led him to the dance floor. She smiled at him – more as a reflex than a desire to please, he thought. As she danced in and out of his arms, her flowery jasmine perfume enveloping him, she pressed her breasts against him – which was only an accident of her dancing move.

They passed in front of the bandstand and Timmons smiled at the band leader, a tall, handsome, mustached sax player, accompanied by a short, bald, grinning guitar player; a weather-beaten, bearded, pale bass fiddler with a sour look and a tubby, baby-faced drummer who shook as he played, like he was having a St. Vitus spasm.

Fast swing music encouraged Timmons to fling himself about, inventing steps, kicking his legs out and in, lifting his feet like he was skipping rope, suddenly raising both arms and wiggling them in the air, then lunging at his partner as if to catch her in a mock embrace.

A GI from one of the tables, seeing him dance with such a

wildly outfitted, colorful woman, smiled at him, nodding his congratulations. The pounding beat, a bombardment of sounds, was repeating its theme like a broken record, while he and his partner were spinning, shaking their hips. The woman, flooding him again with her flower perfume, pressed against him again and as he embraced her she laughed, then suddenly spun away. After the number ended with an amplified blast of sound he and his partner went to the table and sat on a couch.

After resting for a moment she said, "What's happening to you? Are you affected by the *Dia de los Muertos*? It happened to me. I had a dream the other night that I was walking by the creek and heard the whirring of wings but there weren't any birds. I saw a garden with blooming orchids, henbane and hellebore – which were all magical. Then I saw a skull tossed up by the creek water. As I cleaned it off with a rag I realized it was my own skull. I saw a bouquet of dead flowers growing out of a hole in the pate."

He was disturbed by her dream. Breathing easier, he wanted to get back to the dance floor but she went on. "We should worship death as they do in Mexico. You know that in the legend of the *Dia de los Muertos*, there are three deaths: the first is when your heart stops; the second is when you're lowered into earth; the third is when there's nobody living who remembers you."

"Why are you telling me this?"

"Because you may end up in a foreign cemetery. You might be wearing a real death mask."

He was frightened and got up.

"You want to go to my place?"

"No, I have to leave," he said.

She smiled and left the hall, and he returned and found Richard at the writing desk.

"I wasted a whole evening with some witch," he said.

"What was she like?"

"Like death warmed over."

"I wrote a letter to Gloria, and sent her a poem."

"She won't understand it. She never reads anything but comic books."

"Don't be sarcastic."

"Well, I'd like you to see Gloria as she really is."

"And I'd like you to see her as I see her. She's so beautiful. I think of her all the time."

"Well, believe anything you want. I've got to run. I'm going into town to get laid."

Richard finished his letter:

> *Dear Gloria,*
> *It was great to talk to you on the phone, as short as it was. I hope your cold is better.*
> *I think of you all the time. Do you mind if I say you are a most beautiful woman?*
> *Love,*
> *Richard*
> *P.S. I enclose one of my favorite poems*

No beauty doth she miss
When all her robes are on,
But beauty's self she is
When all her robes are gone.

The night before they left for New York, to be shipped to England, their battalion Colonel with Plankton met five hundred select soldiers for a pep talk like the coach's speech before a game.

Richard wanted to trust the Colonel, nicknamed Ramrod – a six-foot red-haired officer with a back like an ironing board and short clipped hair parted in the middle like in the old photos.

They had heard he was being given a second chance, having lost a sizable part of his regiment in Africa through miscalculation. The rumour was that he was too scholarly to be a field commander, that he was better at moving men on a map than getting them through a real forest of enemy soldiers.

From the platform of the Rec. Hall he talked about their coming move overseas and preparations for the trip. Then he said, "In Europe you'll soon be going into combat. And I have to be honest with you. You're going to hate it more than anything you've ever hated before in your life. Now, think of me as your friend. Do you have any questions?"

Richard raised his hand and the Colonel nodded to him.

"As you know, Sir, most of the members of this division were sent overseas as casualty replacements, right?"

"Yes."

"And the soldiers who replaced them here were never given any training as a unit. Now you say we're going overseas to combat. But some of the new guys have never fired a gun."

"I think you're exaggerating, soldier. Everyone in the division has had some time on the firing range."

Richard felt reassured and said, "I'm glad to hear that."

"Any more questions?" the Colonel said.

Timmons raised his hand.

"Timmons," the Captain said, "are you sure it's important?"

"Oh yes."

"Go ahead, soldier," the Colonel said.

"Well, these other guys are afraid to ask."

"What is your question?"

"Well, we're going to England I understand, and we'll probably have a weekend pass to London."

"What's your question?" the Captain snapped.

"Now, when I get off the train I'll be in London. It's not like Georgia where I know my way around. It's strange territory. I want to know how I go about getting a little pussy."

The men roared with laughter. When it died down, the Captain said, "Timmons, you're an idiot."

"No, I'm serious, Colonel."

"Well," the officer said, "just remember – if you have sex,

go to the U.S Army VD clinic. You'll have an exam and they'll inject some anti-biotic in your dick. If you don't have that treatment and you get the clap or syph it's a court martial offense. But on the safe side, you can go to Piccadilly Circus in London. They have English girls at the USO who will dance with you."

"I don't want to *dance* with them," Timmons said, setting off another chain reaction of laughter.

After Ramrod dismissed them the men continued to chuckle and whisper among themselves, forgetting for a time the warning the Colonel had given them about combat.

5

"We have every reason to hope," Ramrod said to the men, fighting a stutter. "We have every reason to hope for success in the battle ahead."

Richard was pleased to hear the Colonel's words.

"We're going to attack," he shouted, almost scaring himself. "According to Intelligence, two German divisions have gone south. Our target, Stein, is only defended by old guys and schoolboys, called *Volkssturm*. They're even greener than you are. With luck, this will be just a practice battle for you. But I don't want you to get cocky. The 7th Armored was supposed to back us up but they haven't arrived. I phoned General Wheeler and he said we'd have to go it alone." He paused for effect. A crust of snow gave way and his foot slid into a hole. He righted himself like a man on a tightrope, lifted his binoculars off his chest and stared into the driving snow, hoping to get an answer from the silent pines. "Visibility is zero," he said, as if by naming it he solved the problem. He dropped his binoculars onto his chest and looked at the assembled GIs whose lives were in his hands. The tone and volume of his voice lowered. "I want to talk to you, man to man."

"Well, I'll be damned," Timmons said.

"Stuff it, Timmons," the Sergeant called over to him.

The Colonel went on in a soft voice – like a father counseling his children about a dangerous task, such as building a raft for a flood. "This morning you're going to make the first strike. It's a grave responsibility. I wish we had good weather. It would be much better if you had your first taste of combat under sunny skies."

Timmons was shaken. He remembered how his boxing coach, Zazz, had warned him that an opponent could punch his lights out. He stared at the Colonel, who seemed miscast in this drama. Timmons' head was a balloon full of questions. Why was the Colonel giving off an air of indecision? Why was the Captain hiding in the rear outpost? Why hadn't the artillery gotten their ammunition? Why was there no aerial reconnaissance to check on the enemy moves? Why hadn't the P-51s come like hovering angels to scatter the enemy for them? What deity had trapped them under this cold white dome?

The snow had sealed them off from other GIs in the company, from other companies in the battalion, and from other battalions in the regiment. Each part of the organization was groping like a blind man for its neighbor on the organizational chart.

What horrified him was the lack of any plan. He knew he would be shot at, but he wanted to be able to shoot back. How could they take a town that was invisible? He thought of all the invisible towns hidden in the blinding snow, stretching from one winding valley to another, up through the Gap – a world in which to practice survival.

The relentless wind swept in and caromed off the assembled troops toward the unseen town below. He was racked by uncertainty, his eyes trying to pierce the mist above the snowy fields, like the headlights of the trucks that had brought him there.

"Are there any questions?" the Colonel asked. "Ask me anything."

Richard knew they weren't seasoned troops, but he was proud to take on German soldiers with years of experience on the Russian front. He wished the Captain was more resolute, who stood uneasy and worried behind the Colonel.

Richard raised his hand – he figured the men expected him to ask a question.

"Go ahead," the Colonel broke in.

"Well, Colonel, a few days ago I saw a German column, a long line of tanks, trucks, and men going south. Headlights were blazing, the trucks were honking their horns. The men were singing. Now, there's a rumor that hundreds of trucks and tanks have moved into Stein. Maybe the Germans are making us think they're going south. But really they're massing their troops right across from us."

"No. According to our Intelligence the Germans have assembled all their forces south of here. We lost fifty men from the 59th Field Artillery south of Auw. Your brothers-in-arms from the 22nd Division are acting like heroes, holding off this last thrust of the German army."

Richard felt that at least the 22nd had done itself proud. He hoped that his division would show what it could do.

Timmons looked at the men sitting in the snow, leaning on their guns for moral support. He heard the sound of wishful thinking – "We'll know more now the fog's lifted," Henderson said. "I'm ready," Rabbit added. "Let me at 'em," Rule said. Other GIs were bolstering their doubts, claiming all would go well when they finally got air support, when the armored units came up, when they got the artillery ammunition. But they didn't fire any questions at the Colonel. Did they think it was better to go to their graves like statues?

Encouraged by the officer's fatherly tone Timmons said, "Colonel, you said we could ask any questions, right?"

"That's correct."

"Well, here's how I see it. The Germans, while making a racket, take a whole regiment south. Then they bring back three more. They take another south, bring back three more. They keep that up until, as Richard said, they have a whole army of troops right across the valley from us, ready to jump down our throats. And there's a rumor we're up against the powerful *Volksgrenadiers*."

"No, as I said before – we're only up against the *Volkssturm*, the home defense units of old guys and young boys."

"Maybe. But the Sergeant told us that in every war the Germans have come through the Losheim Gap. Now, what if they come down now and bring a bunch of *Volksgrenadiers* with them? We've got no air support or armored units. We're an outfit that's never really been trained. We have cavalry men, MPs, cooks – men who haven't fired their guns yet."

"Our planes couldn't get in before. But we're going to do our best. Each fighting man here is a highly trained machine.

We're going to follow our orders like good soldiers. Things are never perfect, the way we'd like them to be. But we're going to do our duty. There will be no retreating."

The men were silenced by the hesitant note in the Colonel's voice and, taking advantage of their confusion, he shouted, "We're attacking Stein! Companies dismissed!"

The Captain gathered his contingent of I Company in an open field. They were to swing west and, joining with K Company, head for Stein. To avoid mines they marched in single file, the first GI taking the risk for the rest. Richard breathed in the cold clear air. They were moving at last. The crisp marble of snow crackled under his boots. What a great day for skiing, he thought. His shoes crunched down on the icy surface, sinking in deep, sucking up the water below.

The line extended across the long field, as straight as men afraid of a mine could make it. Each one hit the same hole full of slush deepened by the man in front of him. The water chilled Richard's left foot, which throbbed with pain.

The thought of a mine made the men quiet. They were awed by the long path they were making in the snow, like a line on a white pad. When they got to the center of the field the snow let up and Richard saw an open patch of blue sky. Suddenly a plane came out of that hole of blue at high speed with another right behind it. The first plane, a Messerschmitt, banked, then came over again. The second, an American P-47, followed and with a burst hit the enemy plane, which caught fire and spun down toward the firs, exploding with orange balls shooting off in a spray. A shout went up from the men, but the Captain waved his hands frantically to silence them.

Richard felt cheered up. If the sky stayed clear they would get more planes to soften the enemy. So far, they could tear out the pages on air support from the manuals. Now, one of their planes had come to help them.

A figure floated down from the sky, swinging from side to side, his parachute billowing out. The Captain sent word down the line for all the troops to have their guns at the ready, in case the German pilot landed near them. The Captain passed Timmons and said, "Gun up, soldier." Timmons raised his M-1 higher and, looking up, saw the German flier disappear into the enveloping woods. The Captain gave the order to lower their weapons.

"Can I ask a question?" Timmons said to the officer.

"What is it?" the Captain replied with annoyance.

"I was at Outpost Two and heard a weird clanking, like a tank track. What do we do if we run into a King Tiger?"

"Timmons, if you didn't ask so many stupid questions and listened, you'd remember what I told you. You call for the cannoneers. They bring up the bazookas to knock out the tank."

"What if they don't come when we call for them? Back in the States we never saw a bazooka."

"If the cannoneers don't come, you call for the tank destroyers."

"What if they don't come? And if a Sherman shows up, it's no match for the Tiger's 88 millimeter cannon."

"Jesus, Timmons, what if the sun doesn't shine? Stop buggering morale with your damn chatter."

At the end of the open field, the P-47 returning, zoomed down to have a look at them. They could race across the field at the mercy of the mines or stay in place and be strafed. The Captain cried, "Stand fast. Show them we're friendly troops." But the P-47 swooped low and let out a burst of machine gun fire, scattering them. The men cursed the pilot, watching him drift off, and they rushed across the snowy path that now seemed a bridge across an ice cliff. How ridiculous the action of the P-47 was, Timmons thought.

He came up to the Sergeant who was staring into the distance as if looking for divine guidance. He appeared ragged, his ODs rumpled like an induction uniform. His face had a new, wasted pallor like the look of an athlete who has reduced too fast.

51

Aware he was in an impossible position he stood motionless, as if asking his Maker for a ray of hope.

"Are we going to attack or not?" Timmons asked.

"I hope you come out of this alive, fellow. After the war you can go home and invent a machine that asks questions all the time. I don't know what we're going to do. Ask the Captain who's hiding somewhere. Ask the Germans – they know what they're doing. An aide to the Colonel just told me we can't get within a mile of that accursed town. They caught a one-eyed German scout, and he said, 'Our Army's coming by the thousands. Get the hell out of here. And take me with you.' But what are we doing? Here we are, grown men running around this God-forsaken pile of snow with our heads up our asses. And let me tell you – the strike's going to come like an earthquake. You'll hear a rumbling like a train coming; then everything'll start flying. But the Lord has His reasons. He'll use me any way He chooses."

They returned to the sand-bagged barricade and Richard noticed the ominous rims of several shell craters dotting the snow banks surrounding their defensive position. He took out his luminous compass and read the bubble levels in the reflected light. When their mortars were set up he and Timmons lay back against the sandbags. A mortar "meanie" screamed over their heads and Timmons' hands began to shake.

"Richard," he said. "They called off our attack because we're in a trap, right? This mountain belonged to them. They can come through those trees with a tank and blast us any time. They could bury us and nobody would find our bodies."

He put his trembling hands on Richard's shoulder. "We're friends, right? I made fun of you college kids. But you didn't hold a grudge against me." He took out the matchbox. "If anything happens to me I want you to have my good-luck charm." He slid out the tiny drawer, revealing a small tuft of matted hair. "It's a gift from Josephine. She said I was a sweet guy and gave me this lock of her pubic hair. If I get picked off, it's all yours."

Timmons slid the drawer back, then put the matchbox in his pocket.

"Timmons, I want to ask you for a favor too. If I don't make it and you come through it all, I'd like you to go see Gloria when you get home. Give her the details of our battle. Don't try to make us out as heroes, but I want her to know what we did. I want her to remember me."

"Sure. I'll do that," Timmons said, then lay back in the barricade and fell asleep almost immediately.

Richard soon heard a sound behind them. Moving quickly to the edge of the woods he left his friend, and scrambled behind a tree for cover.

A sharp, raspy voice pierced the air, "Shirley Temple."

Stunned, he forgot the password.

"Who was the MVP in the American League last year?" the man cried.

"I don't remember."

"Which league are the Cardinals in?"

"The National."

"What player had a candy bar named after him?"

"Ruth."

The speaker came out of the veiled woods – a walking tree, with branches poking out of his field jacket, twigs lining his helmet. "You idiot," he said. "You're lucky I didn't shoot. You know there are Germans everywhere, dressed up in ODs like GIs. Okay, dumbhead, the password for 'Shirley Temple' is 'Walt Disney Sucks.'"

A mortar shell shrieked over their heads and the man raced off into the woods. Richard buried himself in the snowy bottom of his trench and curled up, encouraging the shells to ignore him.

He felt a fire in his throat and drank half of his canteen in a few gulps. His stomach grumbled. It was a novelty not to have anything to eat. He wanted to lie down and imagine a meal. Maybe for a an hour or so he could forget the war – think he was out camping by himself, ready to cook his food over a fire, commune with nature.

Another mortar shell screamed over his head and he stayed low. Then when all was quiet he moved further into the woods but couldn't figure out where the rest of the company was. He looked between two snowy pines and saw a small deserted cabin, probably from the original German defenses. A shell thundered over him and hit the cabin, its roof and two sides peeled apart by the explosion. More shells came burrowing in on the remaining framework as if a hand in the sky were hurling everything at the building.

Smoke poured out of the cabin and Richard heard voices but couldn't tell what language was being spoken. A trap-door in the floor of the room was flung open and a German soldier, bare-headed, came out. In his hiding place Richard lay still, looking over the bushes to see what was happening. The head of the emerging soldier was scorched as though it came out of an oven. A bloody handkerchief covered his eyes. The soldier came all the way out, wearing a filthy grey jacket and long sagging pants. Another soldier, in a muddy black uniform, emerged – an angry man with a curled mustache, a spade in his belt, holding an empty ammo pouch. Another followed – an old officer in a ski cap, with lots of braid on his shoulder. More soldiers came out until there were fifteen or more: men with uniforms ripped open from the direct hit, their chevrons so torn that it was impossible to decipher their ranks. One man with a gash from his ear to his mouth fell down and the man behind him lifted him up and steadied him. Despite the assistance, he fell like a blind man – mumbling and groaning.

Since the rumor was that his division had run out of ammunition, Richard figured the Germans had shelled their own positions.

At midday Richard came to an area he recognized as part of their camp and, lifting his feet over a hedge, stumbled on a body. It was Henderson and, next to him, the body of Watson – the two curled together like boys playing hooky, telling each other stories, mumbling and giggling. He didn't see any wounds. Theirs mouths were wide as if they were howling at some joke. There was new fresh blood leaking out of Watson's left ear, which ran in a river of dirt around the lobe, where he hit the ground. There was also blood around one of Henderson's ears. He figured they both might've suffered a concussion from the same shell. At least they had been together to the end.

He was relieved to run into the Sergeant with Rule and Rabbit. He told them about Watson and Henderson.

"It's terrible," the Sergeant said. "We're getting blasted from all sides. We can't move."

"Let's do something," Rule said. "Come on, Rabbit, let's bag us a tank."

The two ran forward to the hill and Richard went after them until they came to a road between the fir trees where they could look down into Stein. In the distance they heard a low guttural sound. Looking toward the trees, they saw a long cannon poking its stove pipe through the firs. There was a rumbling and then a blast from the cannon's pipe, accompanied by a stream of flame and smoke. A shell exploded in front of them, spraying icicles of the snow's surface.

"That's a German Tiger," Richard said.

"No," Rabbit said. "The Tiger has enormous tracks – it can't come through woods that thick."

"You just saw it take a shot at us," Richard said.

"Let's go for it," Rule said, raising his bazooka. "Come on, you guys."

The three of them moved ahead and the air was filled with the howl of mortars passing over. The crack of machine gun fire came from the direction of the town. They saw the glint of many tanks; the town was teeming with them. Shells began soaring over them and machine gun bullets werc chipping away at the trees. Richard couldn't believe they'd hurl so much at three GIs. Turning to look for the other two, he saw Rabbit was on his back, his legs shorn away, his stomach scaled back the way a fish is gutted, with his blood pouring out. More mortar shells came over, landing near them and Rule and Richard picked up the small man and rushed toward the woods. Coming onto the scene, the Sergeant took charge of the wounded man, ripped off his shirt and tied it around his body.

"What's going on?" Rabbit asked.

"The medic will fix you up," Rule said. "Just relax."

"They'll cut my legs off?" Rabbit asked.

"You lucky guy," Rule said. "You'll get a free ticket out of here."

"Not before I get me a German."

"You won't get one before I do, buddy."

Rabbit fell back as if to sleep, with his eyes closed.

"Work on him, Sergeant," Rule said. "Don't just stand there."

"There's nothing I can do. I just fussed with him till we find a medic."

"Where's the Battalion Aid Station? Let's get him to a doctor."

"It's too late."

"What's going on? Rabbit didn't have a prayer. Who's responsible?"

"I don't know."

"Meanwhile we just sit here and get ticked off like Rabbit."

"We can't move. There's an army of tanks down there, ready to roll right over us."

Rule got up. "I'm carrying Rabbit out of here. Then I'm going after them. I'll blow them skyhigh."

"Stay here," the Sergeant said.

"No," Rule said, and he lifted Rabbit up and swung him onto his back as he would a child. The Sergeant came up to him. "Rule, I know how you feel," he said. "But put your buddy down. I'll show you something."

"No."

"Take his hand, feel his pulse."

Rule grappled with the hand and held the wrist, trying to get the beat.

"He went fast, Rule. Now put him down."

Slowly he persuaded the tall GI to lower his friend and feel for his neck beat. Finding none, he stood over his dead friend. "Rabbit," he said, "What are you doing to me?"

Richard put his arm on Rule's shoulder.

"I'm going in," Rule said. He got up and moved on. Richard, roused by the cut-up figure of Rabbit, joined Rule, leaving the Sergeant behind, who refused to go with them.

From a small rise they saw a field and two roads leading to town.

"I'm going to that field," Rule said. "Cover me, Richard. I'm going to bag me a tank. They've got us zeroed in. We might as well go out firing our guns."

A flare hit the clear sky and Richard froze. But Rule kept going, waving his bazooka like a rifle, determined to fire at anything in front of him. The artificial light hung in the sky and it began to rain 88 shells.

"Freeze," Richard yelled, but Rule didn't hear him and swung his bazooka up as if to aim at this odd moon that washed the field in a pale light. He saw Rule turning and twisting in a weird ballet, his weapon pointed like an artillery gun at the sky. He didn't cry out but fell into the snow and the flare's light dimmed down as at the end of a scene. Richard crawled out in the misty dark to search for him but couldn't find a body in the snow. No one was crying for help. Frustrated, he assumed Rule was dead and, hearing more shells tearing the air above him, he dropped back into a wet abandoned hole.

In the late afternoon he heard whispers from passing GIs that everything was unraveling. The strike against Stein had been blown back all along the line. A heavy fist was coming down on their heads.

"It's just a matter of time," a GI said in the ancient tone of defeat.

If he got through such a monumental collapse, Richard thought, at least it would be over. Once the storm passed on, there would be nothing more coming down on them.

He heard a soft rumble of motors, a slow buzzing of trucks in low gear and he remembered the column he'd seen with the blaring horns and men singing like maniacs. He crawled to the top of the barricade, and he could see a winding column of trucks, tanks and infantry. The Germans weren't going south, they were all moving into Stein. Was that why the attack had been called off?

All night he had trouble sleeping, going over again the enemy subterfuge that had fooled the Colonel and his staff. Yet he felt that now they were being tested. Surely Ramrod would realize their error and set the division on the right course again.

6

To think of something pleasant while lying in a cold ditch Richard thought again of his wonderful visit to Stratford and London with Timmons.

On the bus from Stow-on-the-Wold he had opened the letters he'd received that morning.

Gloria had written:

> *Dear Richard,*
>
> *I was sorry I couldn't talk more on the phone. Father was expecting an important business call. Dad asked about you. He wondered what your financial prospects would be like after the war.*
>
> *How's the action over there? I only know about army life from a Hollywood movie I saw, where a nutty soldier runs around with his head up his butt. Yet maybe military life will make sense to you.*
>
> *One thing I don't get. I should think, with your weak eyes, they wouldn't put you in the Infantry where you have to shoot straight.*
>
> *I'm still having my own shoot-out with Rollo. He doesn't think I have an idea in my head. Just because he's the head-checker at the market he thinks he's uno numero.*
>
> *I saw your mother the other day. A nice lady. She really misses you. She's not happy you're in the worst branch of the army.*
>
> *I enclose a photo you asked for. Rollo doesn't care for the picture but you might like it.*
>
> *I can't write a lot. I'm not a born letter writer. And I don't want you to get any wrong ideas about us.*
>
> *Sincerely, Gloria*

He read a letter from his parents:

Dear Richard,

I see an eighteen-year-old setting off on a great adventure. And we're sure you'll make us proud of you.

Your experience in the infantry reminds me of my days in The Great War. I only served six months and was in the trenches for just two weeks but I'll never forget the camaraderie I had with my fellow soldiers. You'll never forget the buddies you meet in the service.

I found out why General Briggs didn't get you into Officers' Training. He joined General Eisenhower in London as an Adjutant. Now that the invasion has been such a success – despite the unfortunate loss of American lives – Briggs says Hitler will soon be defeated in his final offensive against the Allied forces.

Everything on the home front is going well. I'm working only four days a week and I'm able to play more golf. The Country Club cut down on the number of Entertainment Nights because of the war shortages. But the money we earn from the two Dance Parties goes to USO for its work with the troops.

Many of our local boys are in uniform. You may have heard that Johnny Benton, former captain of the Lehigh football team, was shot down over one of the islands. It's been in all the papers. He's the first real hero and casualty of the war.

Please keep us posted, even though I know it's sometimes hard for you to get letters out from the combat zone.

Mother wants to add a postscript.

Hello, Dicky darling. We think of you so often and hope you are in good health. I wish you weren't in such a dangerous unit but your father says we must get rid of this horrid Mr. Hitler. And you're doing your part. I know you're in a well-trained outfit and will succeed in anything you undertake.

Your dear friends, Elsie and Ted Jones, had a lovely wedding last week at the country club. They mentioned how much they missed you. Mrs. Jones had such beautiful flower arrangements at each table.

Your father and I did a fast swing number with the lively jazz band. I'll send you some pictures, though the photographer caught me in an awkward pose.

By the way the poems you sent to Poetry magazine came back with a rejection slip. I don't mean to discourage you but my friend who teaches at the college says so many people are writing poems and there are so few good magazines to print them.

I met your friend, Gloria, the other day. Such a lovely girl, though her dress revealed too much décolleté. I hope you write to her. She admitted she's a terrible correspondent, which doesn't bode well.

Write soon. We pray for you.
Love,
Mother

They got off the train at Stratford and walked into town.

"I still don't see why we didn't go straight to London," Timmons said.

"Well, I want to see Shakespeare's home. But you can go to London without me."

They walked to the main street where a passerby told them how to get to Shakespeare's place and they ended up in front of the famous building, well-marked as the poet's home.

Timmons persuaded Richard to go directly to a nearby pub. And as they drank their pint of Guinness, Richard stared at the house across from them, as if he was looking at a shrine.

The typical house, with a half-timbered exterior, recalled for him the sketches from his Shakespeare books, though the real house before him seemed to be sinking into the ground.

Shakespeare had lived there, he thought, having the ordinary experiences of a young boy. Richard wondered again how such a person could've come from this common house – the improbable home of a writer, who, his teacher said, had no business writing such magnificent works.

Timmons interrupted his musings, "You really think a lot about this guy," Timmons said.

"Do you realize – he was born and lived in that house."

"I remember reading *Julius Caesar* in high school. What was that about? I forgot."

"It's about whether you can kill someone, even for a good reason. Brutus is Caesar's friend but he was afraid Caesar would become a dictator, so he killed him. But he wasn't meant to be a killer."

"What if we're not meant to kill someone?"

"We're in a good war, fighting the monster Hitler."

"But he's a dictator and you say Brutus was fighting a dictator. Yet he wasn't up to the job."

"You're comparing apples and oranges. Drink your stout. I'm going to see Shakespeare's house and then we'll go to London."

Richard went over to the famous house and was amazed to be entering the comfortable, pleasant living room, with the low oak-ceiling beams, the huge blackened fireplace, where Shakespeare had grown up with his family.

He went upstairs to the poet's birthroom and stared transfixed at another low-ceiling room, and the small fireplace where he imagined the young, unbelievable boy warming himself while dressing for the day.

He bought the brochure at the door which explained everything and returned to the pub, where Timmons was sleeping with his head on the table, having spilled his Guinness on his shirt.

On the way to the station, Timmons said, "Richard, I know you love Shakespeare. But I think you read too much poetry. What do you see in it?"

"Someone said that 'poetry is the language of God.' "

"I remember the first poem I memorized. It was on the wall of a toilet, one of those where you had to put a coin in the slot to open the stall door.

> Here I sit, broken-hearted,
> Paid a nickel and only farted.

"But I guess you wouldn't call that the language of God."

"No. But, Timmy, you can enjoy that graffiti."

"I also picked up this paperback at the station – *Hungry Thighs*. It's my kind of sexy novel. But it may not be your cup of tea."

"No, it isn't. but it'll give you something to read on the train to London."

Richard was excited later to be walking on the streets where Shakespeare, Jonson, and Marlowe had walked. Seeing a line of GIs waiting to get on a bus for a tour, they joined them, getting a seat on the upper deck.

The sun was out and with Timmons resting beside him Richard was thrilled by the sights the driver described over the loudspeaker – the stately Buckingham Palace, Westminster Abbey which he said contained the remains of the famous poets, Chaucer, Browning and Tennyson – the Abbey still miraculously unscathed as yet by the bombing. They passed the ruins of the Parliament buildings. "Only the walls are left," the driver said.

Timmons started a conversation with a pleasant, elderly white-haired woman beside him.

"It's our first day in London," he said.

"We're so grateful you Yanks have come to help us," she said.

"We just went to Shakespeare's house."

"How wonderful for you."

They passed a burnt-out apartment building with one side torn out and the rooms still showing furniture in place.

"I've never seen so many buildings blown apart," Timmons said.

"We've been bombed for many years," the lady said.

"I'm amazed how life goes on during the raids – even musicals and theatre productions."

"My house in Kensington was destroyed. I live now with my sister in Stow-on-the-Wold."

"That's where we're stationed," Timmons said.

"How nice. You must come visit us sometime."

"Maybe you can tell me the best place to find women. I'd love to meet a nice English girl."

"Well, there is Piccadilly Circus. You can dance with the hostesses there."

"Isn't Piccadilly where all the tarts hang out?"

"Unfortunately, there are prostitutes there."

"I'll be frank with you – since you're being so nice. Would you show me around the city?"

"Come off it, Timmons," Richard said.

"Well, I'm just asking."

"I'd love to show you around," the lady said, "but I'm meeting my sister."

"Well, Richard could take care of your sister. We could have some fun."

"Stop it, Timmons," Richard said. "Excuse my friend, mam."

"That's alright. I understand. It's the best offer I've had in thirty years. But, young man, I'm old enough to be your grandmother."

"Well, if you don't mind, I don't mind."

She laughed and said, "I wish I were eighteen and could go dancing with you. But here's my stop. Enjoy the city." She wrote on a piece of paper. "If you or your friend want to have tea with us, here's our address in Stow."

"Thanks a lot," Richard said.

"See you around," Timmons said.

They were passing the Tower of London and Richard remembered how kings and queens were beheaded there. They crossed the bridge over the Thames and were at a stone marker where the driver stopped and said, "Shakespeare's famous Globe Theatre once stood there." Then they crossed the river again, ending their quick tour at Piccadilly Circus. "All GIs should go to the USO," the driver said, "for more information on the sights of London."

Getting off the bus they went to the nearest pub, where Timmons went through three pints, while Richard sipped one.

"Timmy," he said, "I'm going to see a few museums and take in a play. That won't be much fun for you. Why don't we separate and meet Sunday for the trip back to camp?"

"Don't you want to get a few dollies?"

"No."

"You know, Richard, you read about those fabulous women in your books of poetry. That's why you have this hang-up about old Gloria. You need a real woman to find out what they're really like."

"I get sad just thinking about a prostitute. I feel so sorry for her. I just can't treat a woman like a piece of meat."

"You don't understand. When you strike a bargain with a woman, you can drink with her, tell stories and laugh your ass

65

off. She's fun in and out of the sack. You don't know what it's like. I bet Shakespeare rolled in the hay with a few whores."

"And what if I got the clap or the syph and then gave it to Gloria when I came home?"

"I've had the clap – it's nothing to be afraid of. And it's worth it to get that feeling of well-being."

"Well, that's your opinion. Now, meet me Sunday night at the same station, about seven for our return trip."

As Timmons walked off, Richard felt sad that he'd deserted his friend. But they had different interests.

Off Piccadilly Richard found a theatre advertising a murder mystery and bought his ticket for the show which was about to start.

In the first scene an actor named Michael Redgrave was busy preparing a knife to kill his wife, with a long monologue on why he had to do away with her. Half way through his speech there was a loud explosion in the street outside and everyone left the theatre, heading for the shelters.

Richard figured the planes had made a mistake – they wouldn't bomb a theatre. They'd want to destroy a munitions factory. He wasn't going to leave – he'd paid for his ticket and the plot interested him. Would the man get away with the murder?

For two hours he enjoyed the play as the only member of the audience. The murderer got involved with another woman, who by leading him on, allowed the police time to nab him. The point of the play, Richard figured, was that a sensuous woman could lead to a man's downfall.

As he left the theatre he passed the rear entrance to the building and heard someone say, "We had to do the whole play for some dumb GI who wouldn't go to the shelters."

He felt upset but was sure it wasn't Michael Redgrave condemning him.

That evening he found a cheap hotel where he registered, then went for a nightcap before turning in.

He heard the sound of a V-1 put-putting in the clear night sky like a motorcycle and saw the cigar-shaped rocket cross overhead like a fireworks display. And soon he heard its thudding crash on a street somewhere.

He ended up in Fleet Street and found a pub with the delightful name, *Ye Olde Cheshire Cheese*. The place was empty – perhaps, he thought, because the patrons feared an air raid. The bar had a low wood ceiling that seemed to be caving in, making the room resemble a small, deep wine cellar. A framed notice above the bar mentioned that it was the oldest pub in London – where Dr. Johnson once held meetings with his friends.

A young attractive bartender, with a big smile, emerged from a room next to the bar and asked, "What'll it be, Yank?" And Richard ordered a Guinness.

"Nobody here tonight," Richard said. "Do you expect an air raid?"

"You can't tell when the planes will come. We keep the lights down. But you get used to the raids. It's the V-2's that bother me. You don't hear them. They'll just drop on you and take you to the other world."

"You have a good sense of humor."

"You have to laugh at the absurd side of war."

They talked for a bit, Richard filling the young man in on his home in Pennsylvania, and his position in the infantry, which the bartender said was a very respectable one. "I got a release from service," he said, "because my heart keeps skipping beats."

Later a tall, gaunt man came in, with a well-lined face, slightly stooped, just about the oldest-looking man Richard had ever seen.

When the newcomer got his drink, Richard said to him, "I hope I'm not disturbing you. But this is my first visit to London. I can't believe I'm here, in a pub where Dr. Johnson hung out."

"I understand," the man said, in a squeaky voice, grave and funereal, like it was coming from a deep pit. "And Dr. Johnson sat where you're sitting and talked with his friend, Boswell, and the Parliamentarian, Edmund Burke. They solved all the problems of the world here."

"I don't know about Burke."

"He was a great friend of America."

"I'll have to read about him. It's great to talk with you. You're the first Englishman I've met."

"I'm actually American."

"You have an odd accent."

"I've been here a long time. If I may ask, what kind of outfit are you with?"

"I'm in the infantry."

"That's dangerous business."

"Can I ask you a question? Why would Germany choose a monster to run the country – who would bomb England for no particular reason, destroy the historic buildings, like those of the genius Wren?"

"Nobody really has the final answer."

"I've read a lot to understand what's happening. But mainly I read my book of poems which I carry around with me. Do you like poetry?"

"Yes."

Richard took out his book and thumbed through it. "Here are my favorites:"

> Come away, come, sweet love! Do not in vain adorn
> Beauty's grace, that should rise like to the naked morn.

My love and I keep state
In bower
In flower,
'Til the watchman on the tower
Cry:
"Up! Thou rascal, Rise,
I see the white
Light
And the night
Flies."

"Those are lovely lines," the man said.

"I'm so glad to meet someone who likes poetry. Have you ever written any poems?"

"Yes, I have. And now that you mention it, I might ask you for a favor."

"Sure."

"I'm an air raid warden. I spot fires from a roof and relay their position to the firemen. Tonight after watching a raid I wrote a few lines. Would you be so kind as to listen to them?"

"I'd love to."

And he read:

In the uncertain hour before the morning
  Near the ending of interminable night
  At the recurrent end of the unending
After the dark dove with the flickering tongue
  Had passed below the horizon of his homing

"What do you think?"

"I love the dark dove with the flickering tongue. I can see the dive bomber firing his guns down on the city."

"Thanks for listening. Young man, it's been a pleasure talking to you. I hope you get safely through any battles, and return home before long."

He shook Richard's hand and left the pub.

Richard turned to the bartender. "What a nice gentleman – says he's an air raid warden."

"Do you know who he is?"

"No."

"That's the poet, T.S. Eliot."

"My God, I've heard of him. I've read some of his poetry. Imagine – he read some lines from a poem he's working on. That's something to write home about."

Timmons ended up that evening at *The Piccadilly Dance Hall*, where GIs were drinking at broken-down tables in a former bar turned into a night spot for servicemen.

After several whiskeys, Timmons saw a tall girl come in, pretty in a conventional way, with curling red hair, in tight jeans and a loose, revealing man's shirt. Bouncy was the way Timmons would describe her.

She put some coins in the juke box and came over and took him by the hand and led him to the large adjoining dance floor, with posters of half naked movie stars on the walls.

He was delighted to dance with her, wondering why she had picked him out of the crowd of GIs. Two of her friends, dressed casually like his partner, soon joined them on the dance floor and after they introduced themselves, he thought of them as his three pussycats – their hair flowing as they swayed back and forth.

The girls just did their thing as if he were the shadow of a partner. Betty, on the heavy side, with silky bangs almost covering her eyes, was shaking her rear like a showgirl. Jennifer, thin, with dark glasses and a single blonde braid like a dog's tail, moved awkwardly as if practicing steps in a dance class.

He was pleased the three girls enjoyed dancing with him.

"That was fun," Betty said, smiling at him during the break. "It's wonderful to find... a person who likes to go crazy."

When the waitress came to their table he ordered a round of drinks and the girls advised him on the best wine, suggesting the roast lamb for dinner. Leaving them the waitress said, "I saw you all out there dancing up a storm. But don't wear the poor GI out." The girls laughed and Timmons smiled.

Enjoying their wine they talked excitedly about their work. Alma was a high school teacher, trying to make good citizens out of her students – "animals full of testosterone."

Betty was a speech therapist who taught businessmen how to give after-dinner speeches. Her mother and father were vets who recently operated on a sick dachshund. But the animal died and the owners blamed her parents for its death.

Jennifer was a repair woman who restored office machines when they broke down. Her mother was dead. Her father read everything he could find about modern military battles.

"What branch of the service are you in?" she asked.

"I'm in the infantry."

"That means fighting in the trenches?"

"Yes."

"Do you look forward to it?"

"It's the stupidest thing anyone can do. And I'm with an outfit that's never been trained."

"How could that be?"

"There's a saying – situation normal, all fucked up."

The girls laughed and, encouraged by the wine, he dredged up his old repertoire of tales: the story of his youthful sex experience with a Pennsylvania Dutch farm girl; his old account of a drunken student caught in a coed's dorm; and an army joke about a screwed-up private with a French prostitute. He was pleased he could make them laugh.

"I'll bet you have a girl in the States," Alma said.

"No, I don't have one. I like them all."

"I have a question for you," Betty said. "How can you tell if a guy likes you or just wants to play?"

71

"I had a good time with a GI at my place," Jennifer said. "But right after, he put on his clothes, paid me and began listening to a soccer match on the radio."

"I hate that kind," Betty said. "I usually squeeze them so it's over quick. And they think they've had a royal screwing."

"You want to find a guy who treats you right," Timmons said.

"I'll bet you'd treat me right," Jennifer said. "I'll take you on."

"Do you want him?" Alma asked.

"Do you?" Betty asked.

"I've an idea," Jennifer said. "Why don't we all take him?"

"What kind of money are we talking about?" Timmons asked.

"We usually charge a hundred," Jennifer said. "But for a nice guy like you, only thirty dollars."

"That's okay. Where do we go?"

"To my place. Come on, let's have some fun."

At the station next evening Richard looked for his friend but had no luck.

Other GIs from his division walked by, looking worn out and dissipated, their OD's dirty and wrinkled. Richard got his ticket for Stow, found a seat in one of the public compartments and took out his book to enjoy his poems.

Later as he went to the toilet an Englishman stopped him. "One of your lads is in bad shape," he said. "Could you take care of him?"

Richard followed him to a private compartment and once inside saw Timmons sprawled on the floor in front of three disconcerted Englishmen. He dragged him out to the hall and to his place, where Timmons slept until they arrived at Stow. Sick and despondent, he was barely able to walk back with Richard to camp.

A few days later Richard wrote home:

Dear family,

I feel guilty I haven't written more. But I'm never sure my letters reach you.

Thanks Dad, for your encouraging letter.

I had a letter from Gloria. But she admits she doesn't like to write.

I was sorry to hear of the death of Johnny Benton. What a hero. I spoke with him once about his key touchdown in the Lafayette game.

Dad, I often think of your days in the service. I understand how difficult it can be so far from home.

Don't feel bad I didn't become an officer. They need bodies right now and I'm glad to be in the thick of things.

Don't worry about me. I'm with a highly trained division.

I must tell you about my fabulous visit to Stratford and London. We left Stow-on-the Wold, which the guys say means Hole-in-the Wall, but is Old English for Place in the Woods.

At Stratford I sat in a pub directly across from Shakespeare's home. I felt I was looking at a shrine.

While Timmons drank his stout I went across to the house, which was made of stone, with a frame of oak beams. I also went upstairs and saw Shakespeare's birthroom with a low ceiling and a stone fireplace. I couldn't believe I was in his house, which seemed a magical place. Yet I couldn't believe Shakespeare had grown up in such a common, middle class

73

setting.

Then we were off to London, where we took a bus trip and saw Buckingham Palace, Westminster Abbey where the great poets are buried. I saw where Shakespeare's Globe Theatre once stood.

You can't imagine the terrible destruction in the city. We saw apartment buildings completely torn apart on one side with the rooms still visible. But the British are not defeated.

I saw a play with the famous actor, Michael Redgrave – a mystery about a man who murders his wife. During the first act bombs were landing outside in the street. But of course, the Germans wouldn't want to bomb a theatre.

Then at night I had an amazing experience. In a local pub I ran into this fellow, a very old-looking man who was an air raid warden. I found he liked poetry and he read one of his poems to me, about a plane spitting out its fiery flame over London. The bartender told me it was the poet T.S. Eliot.

I enclose a poem I wrote about this.

By chance in an English pub
I met the poet, Eliot
who took a seat at the table
and bending down he seemed
an aged eagle whose wreathed eyes
made him appear
the oldest man I'd ever seen.

I learned he spent his nights
as air raid warden

on a roof above the city
where he heard the dark dove
with a flickering tongue
drop down its deadly load
on burning London.

This famous man
reminded me
the souls of men
are hidden from us –
and give no hint
of greatness
in their common acts
of courtesy.

I'll write more in a few days.
Love,
Richard

7

Richard woke in the morning to an ominous silence. The sun had broken through the mist, making the snow shine. The attack had been postponed. Maybe later they could move on Stein, but they wouldn't have the shield of fog anymore.

A Red Cross courier came by with the mail which he handed out to the assembled, anxious GIs. Richard received two letters but Timmons didn't get any.

"Everything's screwed up," the Red Cross man said. "I can take some letters out but I can't bring any more mail up here."

Richard opened the pink-scented one which was from Gloria and read:

> *Dear Richard,*
>
> *Thanks for your letter. Everything's the same here at home. We have shortages but things are probably a lot worse for you, so why complain?*
>
> *I'm packing fruit for the Allentown Produce Company, which is very boring. I have a backache from lifting crates of apples.*
>
> *I told my fried Jolly about that guy Timmons and she remembered a summer night with him by the lake. I'll leave that to your imagination. She asked you to give Timmons her regards.*
>
> *It's hard to believe you two are buddies. I can't see a guy like you who loves poetry going with Timmons who has such a gross sense of humor. But I guess army life makes strange bedfellows.*
>
> *I don't understand the poetry you sent me. One of the poems sounded kind of kinky. I don't think I'm that hot when my clothes are off.*
>
> *It's great you met Joe DiMaggio. But*

why wasn't he fighting instead of peeling potatoes.

I can't ask you anything because I haven't the foggiest idea what you're doing besides trying to shoot somebody. I've seen a few war movies where GIs are shot and there's blood all over. I don't enjoy such movies. It's so hard for me to believe that human beings are actually trying to kill each other.

I still see Rollo though we fight all the time. I tell him all he likes about me are my breasts. He laughs and says – what's wrong with that?

You're nice but I don't see myself as a beautiful woman. You must get those ideas from all the poems you read. Rollo thinks what you say is funny but he's an insensitive slob.

I wonder if this letter will get through to you. Take care of yourself.

Best,
Gloria

He opened the letter from his family:

Dear Richard,

We got your letter telling us of your wonderful trip to Stratford and London. Mother was very happy that you're able to have some important cultural experiences during your time abroad.

We also read in the papers that it's 40 degrees below zero in the Ardennes woods but I'm sure you're well-protected with your army wool coat.

We laughed at your account of getting your food tossed into your mess kit without your knowing what you're getting. Sounds like they provided you with plenty of good food there.

I know from my own experience that you can't divulge pertinent information on your whereabouts. By this time you probably have fired a few rounds at the enemy's line.

Often in a war there are military failures. But we are heartened by the great success of General Eisenhower in the European theatre. He is embarked, as he says, on the great crusade to bring the Germans to their knees and end this war.

We pray for you and know you'll come out of this experience stronger than when you went in.

Mother wishes to add a note.

Dicky darling, I enjoyed the letter about your visit to Shakespeare's home. I'm sending your account to the local paper. Your friends will love to read about your experiences.

Your poem about finding the photo of a German soldier was hard for me to take. The thought of possibly killing a friend is too frightening. I like my poetry to be cheerful.

And to think you met the poet, Eliot. I'll put that into the news story. I don't understand his poems and the few I've read seem pessimistic – which I hope doesn't rub off on you.

I read your poem about Eliot, but I can't bear to think of London being bombed like that. I'll show your verse to my professor friend to get his opinion.

I knew you'd enjoy the "Power of Positive Thinking." Some GI's only complain about how bad things are but you always find the fruitful experience, even under difficult conditions.

It might sound foolish to tell you to keep warm when dad tells me it's very cold where you are but you have that heavy woolen coat.

Dad says our V-mail letters mustn't be too long, so I'll sign off. Take care.
All my love,
Mother

"I'm sorry you didn't get a letter, Timmy," Richard said.

"The gals I know can't write. What did your family say?"

They're happy about our Stratford and London trip. Mother's sending my account to the newspaper. She met Gloria and thinks she's a lovely girl. My father thinks Eisenhower's great and we're lucky to have him running the show."

"You'd better not tell him what's really going on here. What did Gloria say?"

"She's bored lifting crates of apples. She was amazed we met DiMaggio. And she said your old flame, Jolly, remembers you and sends her best."

"By God, old Jolly remembers me."

"I understand you had a fling with her one summer."

"Yes, we went at it all night. So she remembers."

"You can look her up after the war."

"I might. There's only one problem. She had long dark hair and great boobs like Gloria, but she had those big nose holes that gave her a piggy look."

"Well, I'm happy Gloria cared enough to write. Someday she'll realize what we're doing here."

"She doesn't give a crap about the war."

"Stop knocking Gloria. I'm going to write her now."

He tore a piece of paper from his book and wrote:

Dear Gloria,
I loved your letter. I was sorry to hear of

79

your backache from lifting crates. I hope you're better now.

I know it's hard for you to understand what we're doing here. But we have to rid the world of this German monster.

Gloria, I do think you are a beautiful woman. And I have to ask you – is there a chance you and I might be together after the war? I know it sounds conceited, but once you realize what we've done here, I think you'll be proud of me. And perhaps you might consider becoming my wife.

I carry with me the photo of your lovely face wherever I go.

I can't write any more now.

Love,

Richard

P.S. I enclose a poem I'm writing about you.

Whenever I dream of you
I offer you a crown
and take you to the sea
where you, enticing me,
plunge into the waves
and rise upon the foam
like Venus
from her shell.

He gave his letter to the courier and said to Timmons, "Guess what I wrote to Gloria?"

"You said you loved her more than life itself."

"Cut it out. I asked her to be my – wife."

"Your wife? Oh, no. Remember what we learned in school – 'why buy a cow when milk is cheap?'"

"That's terrible, Timmons. How can you say that?"

"Well, Richard, I'm telling you again – you're wasting your

time with this cowgirl. You never even kissed her. But she rolled in the hay with most of the field hands."

"Stop spreading that dirt. I know Gloria's a farm worker. But she's still the most beautiful girl I know. Okay, I didn't kiss her. But I'll tell you – there was an Italian poet who wrote the greatest poems to his girlfriend, and he never laid a hand on her."

"That's ridiculous," Timmons said, laughing.

"It's only ridiculous to you."

"Well, a bird in the hand is better than one in the bush."

"You're hopeless, Timmons. But we'll see how Gloria responds to my letter."

That afternoon Timmons began humming in his foxhole.

"Quiet," Richard said. "You want to get us knocked off?"

"Don't be a worrywart, Rich," Timmons said. "The Germans are miles away."

There was the airy swish of an incoming shell and Richard threw himself into the snow at the bottom of the barricade and Timmons came flying down on top of him. The shell exploded in front of them and they heard another whistling in. Timmons humped himself into a ball on top of Richard. The shell landed with a deafening crash just in back of them and another shell landed near them among the trees.

The Sergeant, his submachine gun swinging from his neck, came running out of the woods.

"The enemy has overrun all positions," he said. "We were ordered to burn the kitchens."

"I can't believe it," Timmons said.

"You'll believe it when you don't get any chow."

The nerves in Richard's stomach tightened, the adrenaline rolled through him. This surely would be their test. He pushed his gun's safety catch forward. He came to the ridge and looked down. There wasn't any movement. A mortar shell had hit the town – probably one of theirs – and knocked tiles off a roof. He went across an open snow-buried field that was peaceful, aware it might become the setting for a barrage.

The Sergeant, anxious to make one more probe into Stein, gathered his GIs from I Company, including Richard and Timmons. The fog was gone for good and a few scouts coming from the eastern ridges reported all was quiet. Encouraged, the Sergeant had moved them all forward. From a hill they finally got a good look at Stein, the slanting old houses, the cracked chimneys.

"So that's it," Timmons said. "We're fighting for that dinky little town."

The Sergeant stood in the center of his men, red-faced from the exertion of amassing his small band – breathless, effeminate, looking from one man to another like a commander full of a thousand doubts.

"Okay, you Johnnies," he said, "we're going to attack. We have no armored support, no artillery, no air support, no officers, no orders – not even a signal from the heavens whether the Germans have left or not. But the good Lord told me to move our butts. We're going to start our own private war. The Lord be with us. Amen."

"Why rush?" Timmons said. "They say there's a mob of *Volksgrenadiers* down there. Why take chances? They got Groaner, Henderson, Watson, Rule, Rabbit and those three guys from K Company. Let's play it cozy."

"We're going in," the Sergeant said. "We'll find out if the German troops are still there. Come on, men. Remember, we practiced taking a town like this. It's the first step that's the hardest."

Timmons wondered if they were on the edge of a precipice. Was it always like this when you first went into combat? You thought it was too dangerous.

"I'll make the first foray," the Sergeant said. "Who'll go with me?"

"I'll join you," Richard said.

"I'm not volunteering for anything," Timmons said.

Suddenly they saw three Tiger tanks come out of a main street of the town, moving awkwardly, casually, as if going for an outing. The Sergeant stopped, bent low and waved Richard down. A jeep came along the road perpendicular to the one with the tanks, its driver unaware of the danger ahead. As Richard watched, alert to the drama, the jeep, ridiculously small, moved right into the line of fire. The first Tiger, huge and frightening, turned to engage the Lilliputian blocking its way. Two GIs, shocked by the confrontation, leapt out of the jeep. The tank swiveled ahead and crunched the jeep under its treads. One of the GIs had a bazooka which he aimed and fired at the first tank. The Tiger exploded and crashed into a wall.

A Sherman tank suddenly blundered around a corner into the path of the second Tiger. The Sergeant recognized the American tank and, encouraged, raced to assist it, with Richard running to join him. The Sherman, as though amazed by its own presumption, fired, and the second Tiger burst into flames, its turret blown open. Two Germans climbed out. The Sergeant fired at the first, dropping him; Richard fired at the other man but missed. The soldier took shelter behind the last remaining Tiger, which was turning to face the American tank head on.

"Come on," Richard whispered as if to the crewmen in the tank, "fire away."

It was a quiet afternoon in a nondescript town and the scene looked routine to him like a tactical exercise. But this wasn't a sporting contest. The game hadn't been fair – two Tigers against one Sherman. It was unfair that the Sherman had to get in close to blast open a hole in the Tiger's armor. Was that why the American crewmen were waiting to fire?

He cheered on the GIs, "Come on, fire."

The Tiger's 88 cannon fired first, blowing up the Sherman. Machine gun fire from the Tiger raked the area, catching the two GIs from the jeep and spinning them to the ground. No, Richard thought, the Sherman wasn't up to the Tiger except at close range.

The Sergeant had taken off for the woods but the machine gun fire from the Tiger followed and caught him. "I've been hit!" he yelled and Richard ran to him, hoisted him onto his back and stumbled off to the woods, machine gun fire crackling on all sides. He reached the trees, exhausted, drained. The Sergeant was moaning from a neck wound and several hits on his side taken while they were running.

Richard figured he'd have to find a medic. Yet the Sergeant didn't seem to be breathing. Richard felt his pulse but found no beat. He couldn't believe how grimy the man had become in a few short minutes, transformed into a filthy specter encased in mud. And he wasn't breathing.

Richard heard the ominous rattle of the tank and looking back saw the Tiger that had hit the Sergeant, mounting the road toward him. He hurled himself into a ditch and crouched down.

He was alone – the other GIs with Timmons had gone back to the wooded ridge to get away from the tank. He stayed in the hole, uncertain, inhaling the bitter damp air, his foot pulsating with pain. Cut off and threatened by the tank, which had given him nightmares in Basic, he was paralyzed by indecision. It was beginning to snow again, the flakes coming down thick – reminding him of a downpour that had once blinded him on the Vermont slopes, when he'd fallen into a deep crevasse much like the trench he was in.

Hearing the clatter of the tank treads he looked over the edge of the trench and saw the Tiger about a hundred yards off, working its way sideways, like a crab, to get out of the woods and onto the road. Its wide track dug into the frozen limbs of trees, mashing the underbrush, its long canon jerking up and down automatically as if looking for him. The tank nosed up like the one in his dreams. He looked through the falling snow, trying to anticipate the direction the monster would take. The machine edged its way up a slight incline toward his trench. He panicked, left his hole, and ran until he came to three GIs warming themselves at a small fire. "A tank's coming," he said. Hearing the deafening roar, he dove into the watery hole and the other GIs abandoning their guns rolled into the trees for cover.

The machine kept coming, its clanking growing in volume. Richard sighted his gun along the edge of the hole and waited. The tank took on different shapes as it bobbed and maneuvered the rocky terrain. Looking over the top of his trench he saw the long slender stove pipe of the 88 swing up to the sky and then down toward him. He imagined an eye inside the tank searching him out like a trapped animal. He released his safety catch, raised the barrel over the edge of the trench, aimed at the tank and fired. The tank slowly eased around in his direction, its 88 snout sniffing him out. He shot again, bouncing a few shells off the forward armor and kept shooting until his clip was empty. A blast from the tank hit the branches around him and he felt a stinging pinch on his shoulder. He moved quickly out of his hole, spinning by reflex into the brush like a lizard, his hands and neck torn by the branches, his arm instinctively over his helmet as pieces of shrapnel rained down from a tree and hit him in the chest like the kick of a horse. He heard himself scream.

He had imagined it all ever since he'd seen the training films of the King Tiger. He'd asked again and again what he should do against the tank and they'd laughed – officers and GIs. Now, blood soaking his shirt, he knew that with all the bazookas, there wasn't much you could do against a Tiger.

But to his relief he heard the tank's booming voice off in the distance.

Lying deep in the earth, he had an itching sensation in his shoulder and had the feeling an animal was gnawing away at his chest. After each bite, there was an echoing pinch in his back as the pain was relayed from front to back like an electrical current.

His glasses were gone and he now saw things through a filmy haze.

Who was responsible for his helplessness? Who had put him at such risk?

With such questions he passed an eternity in a few hours. Later the snowfall stopped and for a time he dozed off. When he woke, a medic was crouching over him, solicitous, pulling at his jacket, loosening his arms, taking his jacket off. He ripped apart Richard's shirt and unwound the shreds from front to back. From a kit he took a pad and cleaned his shoulder with a disinfectant, then bandaged the wound. Asking Richard to lie back he cleaned his chest and wrapped strips of adhesive around his front and back to hold the gauze in place.

"How are you doing?" the medic asked.

"It's like something's eating away at my chest."

"I fixed your shoulder wound," the medic said. "The shrapnel split the bayonet you had on your backpack. That must've saved your life. It's on the ground – you might like it for a souvenir. I took a few pieces of the shrapnel out of your chest. I didn't see any more but I don't know what you're hiding. We're not far from the Battalion Aid Station but nobody knows where the doctors are now since the German breakthrough. Ramrod and his gang are over there in the ditch across from us. Everything's coming apart. I've got to haul ass. I've done all I can for you, buddy. Try to find one of our medics as soon as things settle down."

"Thanks."

Without his glasses Richard watched the man crouch low and move off as in a dream, merging into the anonymity of the woods. Looking around, Richard just made out men crawling into holes on all sides of him. Every company had GIs congregating on the hill, stretched out, wounded and half frozen in their holes, unattended.

A roar of tanks came from the opposite hill and before the machines appeared, a crowd of GIs walked into the area with their hands up, silhouetted against the sky: an unending stream of them, stumbling, disheveled – the wounded supported by friends, the dying finding places on the ground.

The army of King Tigers came into view on the hill.

Unaware of the arrival of the tanks, a truck full of GIs

rounded a bend in the road and one of the Tigers opened fire and the truck burst into flames – the GIs hurling themselves out the back, one of them yelling, his clothes and hair on fire. A GI, after hitting the ground, raised a carbine and fired at the tank. "Don't fire," someone shouted – an American officer, Richard figured. One of the Tiger crews, alarmed by the sudden arrival of the truck and fearing more resistance, shot a blast into the trees behind Richard. A hail of shrapnel sprayed the area, forcing all the men with raised hands to hit the ground. "Stand up and keep your hands high," the American officer shouted. The GIs on the ground got up, their hands in the air. So many giving up, Richard thought. A Tiger taking the lead pulled up behind a line of surrendering Americans. A revolver shot rang out from the ditch where the officers were dug in. "Don't fire," the officer shouted. But as if the gunshot was a signal, the tank crew in front of the line of GIs opened up with machine gun fire on them. Several tanks on the hill joined in and blew shells into the huddled men with their hands up.

Richard kept his head down and heard the screams of the stricken GIs who were figures in a shooting gallery, going down one by one as the tanks on the hill fired in unison.

No, no, he thought, not all of us.

A German noncom leapt out of the lead tank, lifted his machine gun and sprayed all the wounded backward and forward as if he was hosing a garden. The groans died down and finally it was quiet.

A flare shot up above the trees and a shell exploded in the distance. Ramrod and two of his officers dove into a ditch near Richard. A litter passed the Colonel's trench with an officer from I Company, half of one leg gone, with blood gushing onto the snow.

A few men were still wriggling snake-like, twisting in pain, entangled with other blood-spattered bodies.

Why, Richard wondered, had the Germans fired at the hundreds of GIs who had given up, their hands in the air?

The enemy troops disappeared into the woods, unaware there

were still GIs alive in the ditches. Ramrod and his men scrambled away from the deadly region as if they didn't know where they were going.

Richard stumbled off to get back to his Company.

8

For a few days nothing happened and the men were restless. Then one morning the Captain suddenly came up to the line, and Timmons, as if speaking for the others, asked him, "Captain, when are we going to attack?"

"We can't get close to Stein – it's full of tanks. We're being mauled. The Colonel doesn't know what to do. He's running around like a chicken with its head off. He ordered me to come up here and find out what's happening so we can reorganize for a new attack. I said he'd have to come too but he claimed he was needed in the rear. He said he'd court martial me if I disobeyed."

"Are we going to attack or not?" Timmons asked.

"How the hell do I know? We're getting hit from every direction. How are you doing, Richard?"

"Some medic patched me up. I feel okay."

"He caught some shrapnel from a tank," Timmons said.

"Somebody's going to pay for this," the Captain said – "the Colonel, or the General."

A jeep came down the path from the woods and the Captain called out, "Hold on there." The driver stopped. "All of you, get in the jeep – Timmons in front, Richard and me in back."

"What're we doing?" Richard asked.

"We're going up that road."

"No, we aren't," the driver said, a nervous Corporal with a long face. "We don't go up that road. The Germans have control of the hill."

"Take us up," the Captain said. "That's an order."

"You heard the man," Timmons said. "We don't go up that way. There's a ton of Germans waiting for us to make a dumb move like that."

"I've been up there," the Captain said. "There aren't any Germans. And we're going to prove it. I told you – we're the eyes of the regiment."

"I'm not going," Timmons said. "But you can go right

ahead."

The Captain took out his pistol and pointed it at Timmons, "Get in, hotshot. That's an order. And I'm not afraid to use this."

Shaking his head Timmons climbed in front with the driver; Richard and the Captain got into the back.

Cursing under his breath the driver shifted into low and moved up the hill. He drove a few hundred yards when a German soldier came out of the woods, waving his rifle at them like he was hitchhiking a ride. He did this so fast it scared the Captain who dropped his pistol. The German Corporal, a heavy-set man wearing glasses, motioned for them to drop all guns on the road; then he hit the driver's helmet with his gun butt, urging him to drive on. The Corporal drove slowly up the rise, with the armed German walking alongside, escorting them.

The Captain had taken off his helmet so that his long blond hair fell down like a woman's. He was fumbling with his wallet, looking for his papers and, Timmons figured, for his officer's ID.

Timmons stared at the officer and said to him softly, not wanting to upset the German, "You royal piece of shit. What will people say when they hear I'm a POW? You take us up the hill like Jack and Jill and we all come down as prisoners. So help me – when I get back I'll piss on your grave."

The Captain was silent.

Coming to the top of the hill they ran into a group of German noncoms around a truck, with three captured American officers in the back. It was all unreal to Timmons as if he were looking at a movie. The German soldiers bore little resemblance to the dangerous figures of his imagination.

The Captain jumped out of the jeep, some of his papers falling onto the front seat and the Corporal who had captured them waved his arms for him to stay where he was. "*Steig ein,*" he shouted. But the Captain refused to stop and moved towards the Americans in the truck, shouting, "I'm coming with you."

The noncom looked confused but then screamed at him, "*Schwein, steig ein!*"

"Nein," he shouted back, shaking his head as if in a dream of heroic action. Waving his papers in the air, pointing to the Americans, he shouted, "I am an officer. I go with the officers."

The German took out his pistol, ran up to him, and shoved the weapon against his head. The officers in the truck stared at the drama. "*Steig ein,*" he repeated and the Captain got back into the jeep. The Corporal ordered the driver to move on with Richard and Timmons, keeping his gun on them as they moved slowly over the hill – coming to German controlled territory and a field where American prisoners were assembled after the collapse of the division.

Richard and Timmons joined the gathered POWs and ended up near Ramrod and his staff.

"Did we have to throw in the towel, Colonel?" one of his aides asked, –a heavy set Major, too fat for any quick moves.

"What could we do?" the Colonel said. "They screwed up at Supreme Headquarters. They thought we were fighting *Volkssturm*, old guys and schoolboys. But we were up against *Volksgrenadiers*, thousands of crack German infantrymen. We lost all our guys because, as General Bradley said, he didn't know German."

"It's one for the books," an aide said.

"I heard on short wave that Eisenhower ignored the warning from Intelligence about this massive attack. While we were being decimated, he was celebrating his Fifth Star at Versailles, drinking champagne with his girlfriend."

"Well Colonel, there's enough blame to go round. I'd like to get my hands on Whistling Willy. I understand he abandoned all of us."

"They say General Wheeler had a heart attack."

"Lucky for him. He's the only one who got out of this trap. The son of a bitch is probably all the way to Paris by now, claiming he's the hero of Ardennes."

"Well, right now make sure all the men get rid of their weapons."

One of his subordinates looked angrily at the Colonel and swung his M-1 against a tree. The Captain came up to the Colonel's trench and, hearing about the order, unslung his grenade pouch and poured the grenades onto the ground; then he lifted his carbine and cracked it against a fir, where the gun discharged, and he let out a cry, holding on to his injured leg.

A tall wiry German Private, wearing dark glasses and waving a pistol, rounded up all the GIs as if it had been a game the Americans had lost and he was saying, "Well, that's it, that wraps it up." The Private looked like the average bread-and-butter German soldiers they'd seen in training films, doing his duty, killing as efficiently as he could, just like he'd cut down trees, without heroics, just crawling through the brush, moving up hills and down valleys, obeying orders, knowing how to fire accurately, repair a gun if it misfired, or bayonet an American if his gun failed.

The soldier checked the Americans for guns and, finding none, waved his pistol at them to line up. The Captain emerged from the woods, approaching the tall figure and said in the voice used to talk to foreigners or children, "I am a Captain. I want to go with the officers." The man waved him into the line.

"How're you doing?" Timmons asked Richard.

"I've got a weird sensation in my chest. But I'll make it."

Two more German noncoms came out of the woods as if on cue and took charge of the prisoners, signaling with their weapons for the GIs to move down the road. Richard had to rush to keep up with the guards who set a fast pace. His left foot throbbed from the frostbite; his toes felt sore and cramped in his soggy boots. As he walked off he felt the bubbling sensation again in his chest.

"Can you believe what happened?" Timmons asked.

"We were overwhelmed by numbers," Richard said.

"We had no business being here in the first place – some of our guys never fired a gun. And we only lasted a couple of weeks."

"We're lucky. We could've been massacred like the others."

A plane came over – it looked like an American P-51 – and the POWs stood in place and waved their arms to indicate they were Allied soldiers. But the plane swept down on them and dropped a bomb, forcing them to fall flat on their faces in the snow before it exploded at a safe distance.

"The bastard," Timmons said. "Didn't he see us waving at him?"

When they got up they headed down the hill into Stein. Along the way they joined a line of GIs with bandages on arms, legs and heads, stumbling along, their friends holding them up.

They walked past American machines abandoned on the road: tanks, half-tracks, trucks, and jeeps. Rifles, bazookas, mortars, and masses of leather equipment had been tossed onto the snow.

Word was passed from one GI to another that the division had been wiped out. They spoke of a screw-up beyond their wildest imaginings: "I never fired my gun," "Fucked up officers," "I hear thousands were captured," "I'd like to get hold of our General – Whistling Willy."

On the road Richard ran into two men from his company. "We heard you were wounded," one said. Timmons put his arm around Richard's waist, helping him as they walked, as if their new roles made defeat palatable.

"I'm glad you're okay, buddy," Timmons said.

Richard realized his wound set him apart, gave him a special redeeming ticket, now that he entered enemy territory.

As he walked toward Stein, without his glasses, he saw everything in a vague haze: enemy trucks, cars and half-tracks, nose to tail, their mission accomplished. A crew of five Germans in the back of a truck were celebrating, passing around a bottle of wine.

At the top of the hill which led into Stein the GIs in the lead slowed their pace, apparently to look at something Richard couldn't see yet. Slowly they continued down the opposite side of the hill. When they reached the top they saw a dead GI frozen in a field, his head hanging down, his body leaning forward against a fence as if he were trying to keep from falling. Coming alongside the body, Richard saw that it was Rule; his chest and arms had been wired to the fence, like a scarecrow. He had his arm up, shaking his fist at the unknown forces responsible for his humiliation.

Later, in the afternoon, as they passed through Stein, the object of their attack, the prisoners felt humiliated. Had they done everything possible to take the town? Would they be blamed for giving up so much territory without a fight? Now, they realized, another division would have to fight for the region – the main spigot for all German Troops pouring onto the western front.

White flares floated down on the dying town, implying the start of a raid. Soon bombs began hitting the outskirts. A blue flare rose up over the river and they watched as the rain of bombs came closer.

An enormous black cloud rose from the town and out of the cloud came a huge snowball of fire, gathering strength like the sun, heading toward their hill. Stein was receiving its death blow from an armada of planes in the air. More bombs came crashing onto the fields around them and Richard felt waves of heat pouring over him, burning his chest as the firestorm spread out, obliterating the town, sweeping the boards clean.

Domburg

9

After their long hike that morning Richard looked down into the valley and vaguely made out the town of Domburg, spotted with stone houses so old that they seemed, even at the distance of several miles, to be sinking into the ground. Their uniform chimneys shot up like sticks, the wisps of smoke curling from them uniformly too, like the spirits of departing citizens.

But it was the decaying wooden barns leaning forward like old men – one even bearing a swastika on the face like a Pennsylvania Dutch hex sign – that made him think of the farms outside his home.

The town was hardly worth a tourist's visit, yet it fascinated him. It was his home till the end of the war, however long that would be. Behind him was the burning town of Stein, the object of their hate. Behind him were the artillery guns and shells that could arbitrarily fall on his head. He had nothing to fear from them now. He was out of their range of concern. How weird it was. He had entered the snow-blinding woods on his side of the front, met his tank and received his badge of a wound. The change from soldier to POW had come fast as though a wand had passed over his head, transforming him. And now he had broken through into the enemy's world on the other side of the front, as if he'd broken through a two-dimensional painting of the war.

He was exhausted. The long march from Stein had been an endurance test. The marchers in the front lines set the pace and everyone wanted to be in the first rank to set the rhythm, so the space between the marchers altered as more from the back raced to get to the front, and those left at the rear, with bad feet like Richard, stumbled along, trying to keep up with the others. Then a guard would force the POWs back into rows of five, sending the newcomers back to the rear and the process would start all over again. All day long there were some continually running, raising their feet high in the snow to keep up with the accordion-like change in the march.

The ration for the march was a sixth of a loaf of stiff pumpernickel and two slices of hard, tasteless cheese. Timmons divided his sixth of a loaf into seven hunks so as to have something to munch on throughout the march.

They had a scare the night before, on their last lap to Domburg. Richard recalled they'd passed a signpost with an arrow marked *Westerwald*, which, he figured, meant they were entering a western province of the country. When they came to an isolated village they were taken by the guards to a small, lovely chapel with a large stained glass window of Adam and Eve in the garden, that covered the entire façade. The officers were billeted in an office with a fireplace; the others, including Richard and Timmons, took pews in the nave. Later the American officer in charge told Timmons he could stay in the office if he kept the fire going. All night they heard him hacking away at the logs, the heat from his fire becoming so intense it spread to those in the pews.

In the morning Richard woke to the pounding above his head and saw Timmons' axe slicing through the boards. Having run out of logs, he was chopping down the walls for firewood.

The officer in charge, warmed by Timmons' labors, had slept like a dead man during the demolition job on the chapel. When he woke up and saw the results he panicked. Everyone was in the same room, officers and enlisted men; the gem of a medieval chapel was in ruins; a thick tapestry of Biblical scenes was ripped in two; and a cubist-like painting of an angry Job lay shredded on the floor.

After cursing Timmons with a rare display of obscenity, the American officer held an emergency conference with the other officers. They decided to persuade the guards that they should all move out before dawn so they could get far from the village before the morning raids. The guards, who had been drinking all night, didn't object and ordered all the POWs to hit the road. They were several miles beyond the village – crossing the small river, Lahn – when Richard realized again that they might've been shot for desecrating a holy shrine.

Richard thought of the near disaster when he came to the outskirts of Domburg and saw another small church on a hill, like the obligatory town church from the tour books – a squat Gothic structure with unmatched spires – hovering over the houses below like a disdainful priest. A nun, red-faced, slapping herself for warmth, came out of a church door and waved a blessing at the guards, shaking her head at the Americans, blaming them for the people's suffering. Richard hobbled along, favoring his sore foot, occasionally feeling the pinch from his shoulder bandage and an irritation from his chest wound. Yet he was happy to be able to walk, imagining in the cold crisp air that he was on the way to a winter football game. The pain in his chest had subsided, thank God.

He looked about him at the smashed houses with their roofs torn apart, apartment buildings chopped in half, a road carved up as with a knife, a field uprooted by the ploughing bombs. Without his glasses, it all appeared to him like a surrealistic painting. Yet German civilians were starting their day. An old man went about wheeling a cart; a woman, her scarf muffling her head except for her eyes, returned from a store with packages of food; a mother at a gate called to a young girl to come inside as if the prisoners might harm her child.

They passed a building with officers working inside a window, the word *stadtpolizei* on the door outside, which they figured meant "police station." In the main public square a bronze World War I soldier stared at the sky with blank, patina-green eyes.

Richard saw the blurred face of a young woman in the window above a butcher shop, her long hair falling onto her shoulders and he recalled the dream he'd had about Gloria, cradling his head, caressing him, then wriggling like a fish that he'd caught.

A man and a woman came out on the porch and stared at them. "They all come out and look at us," Timmons said. "It makes them think they're winning the war."

The slight fog over Domburg lifted and they saw fires

smoldering from the previous day's bombing. A cloud of dark smoke blew toward them from Stein. At the top of a hill a castle with a black flag on its turret was burning. The sky to the east was red with flames from the daily raids with searchlights poking white fingers into the air.

A Tiger tank clattered out of a barn door onto the street, no longer a nightmare threat to them, accompanied by a Corporal drinking from a huge pitcher. A truck pulled out from beneath a tree, packed with German soldiers in stone-grey uniforms, sitting rigid in their seats as if ready for a parade. Another truckload of troops moved out of a ruined farmhouse that had only one wall that remained standing.

The tanks, trucks and supply vehicles drove through the narrow streets. An artillery piece rolled out of a backyard without disturbing the clothes on a line. An armored car backed out of a churchyard, an officer erect on the back seat. Timmons could see the piping on his cap, red patches on his collar, the imposing Iron Cross around his neck. Two soldiers seated on top of the hood of a small truck stared at the GIs on the road and one gave Timmons a mock salute.

The huge force had materialized out of its camouflaged setting. These were the soldiers he would've met if he'd stayed in combat. Was there no limit to German material, tanks and men? Had the Germans such power even with the crippling losses on the Russian front?

As quickly as they had appeared the enemy soldiers and their machines left for the front. Richard felt that he was backstage watching the actors move up for the next scene.

They trudged up one last hill and, coming over the crest, they got a panoramic view of the Domburg *stalag* and the railroad yard, with several huge warehouses along the tracks. To the west they all got a clear view of the wreck of a three-storied hospital on the adjacent hill – a deep crater carved out of the center of the building and traces of the thick red points of a cross, like streaks of blood, on the jagged roof. A B-17 fortress had made a perfect bull's-eye on the cross, an ominous sign for the POWs. A plane with a black swastika swept over them as if leading them to their new home.

At the gates of the *stalag* the officers were let in but the others were turned away. The camp was packed, they were told, with thousands of POWs coming in from the disastrous Stein battle. Richard and Timmons had to settle for an enormous green warehouse in the repair yard.

They went through the door of the warehouse and Richard, hardly able to see without his glasses, stumbled on bodies packed together on the crowded floor. They found places in a rear section of the room that had buckets of lye against the wall. Richard took the low bunk and Timmons the middle one of a wobbly three-tiered bed.

"What lovely quarters," Timmons said.

"At least we have a bunk," Richard said.

A foul odor came down on them from a POW on the top bunk of their bed, who, shifting about on his wire mesh, sent a rain of straw down on them. That evening Richard stretched out on his coarse straw bedding and was asleep in an instant.

He dreamt he was ringing the doorbell back home, late at night. Nobody came to the door. He tried his key but it wouldn't turn the lock. A light finally came on inside; there was someone shuffling about on the other side of the door. "Who's there?" a gruff voice called out. "It's me, Richard," he said. A small, hinged viewer was yanked to one side; its wire screening made it appear the person was looking out at Richard from a prison cell. He saw an unbelievably ancient face enshrouded in a white head of hair and white beard. It was his father. "It's late," he said in a hollow hoarse voice. "You should've come sooner." He banged shut the viewer and went back into the inner recesses of the house. Richard rang the bell again but there was no response. He walked around to the rear and let himself in the barn door. It was musty and dark but he found a pile of dirty straw and lay down, cold without a blanket, feeling like an outcast, wondering why his father hadn't opened the door. Anyway, he was home. In the morning he would go back to the main house and identify himself to the family. They wouldn't abandon him forever.

Waking up in the morning Richard heard voices tumbling down from the upper bunks around him or drifting from the middle shelf of one bed to the other along the row on row of three-tiered beds. He tried to make out the odd faces, unshaven, peering out at him from the slots of the beds. Men were stretching or sitting up with their feet dangling down; others lay back-to-back on the floor, jammed together like fish on their parcel of straw.

Timmons, above him, was awake, slowly realizing where he was and the first wave of depression rolled over him. He was a prisoner. And what had he done to be incarcerated in such a dump?

"Tea!" a GI on duty shouted from the center of the warehouse and the man on the top bunk held his mess cup over the side of the bed as if begging Timmons for a handout. "Get my tea!" the man said.

"Don't get it for him," a man shouted from the bunk across from Timmons. "Nutzel's afraid to move – because he's got a plate in his head."

"I'll put a plate in your head," the man replied. And Timmons saw the face come over the edge of the top bunk – a prematurely old man in a knitted balaclava cap, with a dirty beard and sunken eyes, his head circled by a dirty white bandage like a boxer wrapped in a towel.

He pushed his cup toward Timmons who took it and got in a long line with Richard – which wound through the crowd of bodies to the huge can at the entrance. They walked by a window and Timmons saw the skeleton of an apple tree and the watchtower where a soldier stared down at them. They filled their mess cups at the can where a guard called Dewey ladled out the morning tea – a one-armed veteran with two faded medals and a silly mustache that reminded the POWs of the New York governor. "Fuck you," the guard said to each prisoner, making the POWs laugh – a greeting they had told him meant "good morning."

After tea the *stalag* commandant, Axel, came in, a huge man puffing in his greatcoat, with grey hair cut short and even like a hedge. Seeing the officer, the guard, Dewey rushed to the rear and slid under a bed, his sleeve without an arm hanging out until he yanked it under. "Corporal!" the commandant boomed out, "Corporal!" The GIs, their sympathy with the underdog, were quiet and finally the officer gave up, grunted and left. Dewey came out to mock applause, dusted himself off, looking embarrassed, ashamed at avoiding some duty.

Richard and Timmons found the mint tea warmed their insides. They sat back in their bunks, content, despite the stench of lye in the room. A guard began hanging green cloth over the windows to camouflage the building for the daily noon raid.

Nutzel, drinking the tea Timmons got for him, looked at Timmons who still wore the Lion insignia on his arm.

"So you're the boys from the Golden Lion outfit?" he said. "You cowardly lions lost all the ground our guys died for."

"We ran into three divisions of *Volksgrenadiers*," Timmons said. "We had no air support, no armored units, no artillery. And I'm here because of a screwed up Captain."

"I heard thousands of you lions threw in the towel."

Had it been a shameful capitulation? Richard wondered. Had they failed their test? How would he explain it to the people back home? Well, it had been a tremendous onslaught against their green division.

"What's the report?" a voice boomed out and they saw the medic come in – a fat Englishman, with a full beard that hid most of his small face, except for his eyes that looked like deep holes cut out of a pumpkin.

"Drop your cocks and grab your socks," he said with good cheer.

103

"Blow it out your ass, old chap," Nutzel shouted as if it were the standard reply to the medic's greeting.

Richard, falling in line for a checkup, walked by a beam with a mirror nailed to it and tried to make out his face, which was dark like a miner's. His chin was black with dirty bristle and his clothes were greasy, giving off a straw stench.

The medic gave him the standard tin of ointment for his frostbitten foot and put bandages on his shoulder and chest. "Your shoulder's almost healed," he said.

"How's my chest?"

"A good question," the Englishman said. "You say you were hit by fragments from an 88 shell. You might have a piece left in your chest. We need an X-ray and we can't get one, not even at the *stalag*."

"Should I exercise?"

"If it's healing, you want to keep moving. If it's not you've got a bomb waiting to go off. Move around and you activate it. Remember what the poet said: 'The brave man runs till he falls; the coward lies down and dies.'"

Checking the bed cases the medic found a dead GI across from Timmons. "Well, here's a man who's flown to a better place," he said. "Can I have a couple of volunteers?" Timmons helped another GI wrap the body in a canvas sack and carry it to the entrance.

"What killed him?" Timmons asked.

"A fever," the medic said.

"Bullshit, you English quack," Nutzel called out.

"Now chaps, be fair," the medic said.

"What really killed him, Limey?" Nutzel asked.

"It's the disease we call mortality," the medic said.

"He didn't eat, you asshole. He didn't have a banquet every night like you Limeys."

"We get the same rations as you Yanks."

Nutzel came up and grabbed Timmons. "He's not dead."

"A friend of yours?" the medic asked.

"Yeah. And he's not dead. You're not a doctor. Leave him

104

here."

Two GIs near the entrance held Nutzel back so they could take the dead man out. Timmons helped them dispose of the body in a waiting truck outside and then went back to his bunk.

"Attention!" someone called out from the front office.

In the light from the half-opened door Richard made out their company officer.

"It's the Captain," Timmons said. "We can't shake him."

"Listen, you new guys," the Captain said, limping as he came in, still bothered by the self-inflicted wound to his leg. "The *stalag* hospital was blasted two nights ago as you could see when you came in. Hundreds of GIs were killed. German doctors and nurses were buried alive. Commandant Axel isn't too friendly with us right now. If any of you strike a match when the bombers come over, the guards will shoot at it. And don't think of escaping. They'll take revenge on all of us if any wise-ass tries to break out."

"What's on the menu today?" Nutzel asked.

"You'll get a boiled potato and hot tea."

"What about bread?"

"There's no bread because of the bombing of the hospital."

"What about Red Cross food packages? Where are you hiding them?"

"There aren't any."

"I hear they get parcels over at the *stalag*."

"You're hearing things. Now I'm trying to make it easy for you people so you don't have Germans riding your ass. You new guys better stop feeling sorry for yourselves. Look at your clothes – they're filthy. If you want to survive start picking the lice off your balls. Nobody's going to do it for you."

When the Captain returned to his office, Timmons asked Nutzel, "Has anyone ever tried to get out of here?"

"Yeah. A bunch of hotshots last month took off at night, went a hundred miles through the snow. Every civilian had a gun ready to pop off at them – every mailman, every bus driver. A mayor of a town caught them in a barn, beat the hell out of them. And they had to walk a hundred miles back. A couple got terrible frostbite: one lost most of his toes; another guy lost both feet. You can be a hero and walk a couple hundred miles if you want to. I've done all the walking I'm going to do for the next hundred years."

Later in the morning Nutzel asked Richard and Timmons to help him look for fire wood for the stove and they went by a small yard filled with dirt and garbage, where prisoners were walking around in sandals, their filthy skin showing through the holes in their torn pants and shirts. One had a black tasseled fez on his head and wore light khaki tropicals. Most wore baggy trousers fastened at the ankles. There were British helmets with forked chain straps, heavy American overcoats and remnants from the uniforms of the Italian Liberation Corps.

"Who are they?" Timmons asked.

"They're deserters from Mussolini's ragamuffin army," Nutzel said. "But they wouldn't fight for the Allies, so they have no protectors. They can be starved or shot any time."

Nutzel took a prune out of his pocket and held it up like a prize, waving it in front of the man with the black fez, like a magician who might make the object disappear. The Italian pushed his hands through the wire and Nutzel tossed the prune into the air as if making a baseball pitch and it fell in the dust of the compound. The man with the fez and several other POWs threw themselves at the ground to get the prize, piling on top of each other. Nutzel and other GIs at the fence roared with laughter.

"What a riot," Timmons said.

"That's vicious," Richard said.

"They take what they can get," Nutzel said. "I got these prunes from a guy at the *stalag*. Nobody wants them – they give you the shits."

Nutzel took them across the tracks beside the warehouse to a place he said had plenty of kindling. Favoring his sensitive foot Richard crawled with the others through a hole in the wire fence between the American and Russian compounds, coming out in front of a deteriorating brick building that had cardboard windows like condemned buildings he had seen in the slums back home.

"They said they'd shoot anybody going into the Russian compound," Nutzel said. "But it's so stinking, the guards have stopped patrolling." They went into one of the buildings and Richard smelled a foul odor like diseased flesh that made them nauseated. Nutzel scurried about, encouraging Richard and Timmons to pick up pieces of cardboard that had once been taped to the windows but now lay shredded on the floor. Bodies were lying in the three-tiered beds. The Russians seemed to be sleeping, though it was morning, lying on their backs with blankets up to their necks the way corpses are prepared for viewing.

They got enough cardboard for the fire. Before leaving, Nutzel pointed to the rear beds. "You see those guys sleeping in the bunks. They're stiffs. A Russian dies; his friend pulls the blanket up to his neck so they can count him for bread. They keep a whole roomful of sleepers, to count off for the guards. 'There's three of us,' a Russian tells the guard. 'But don't forget old Ivan snoring like a trumpet there; he makes four. And there's Dmitry sleeping on his money; he makes five. There, praying in the cobwebs is Alyosha – number six. Also groveling in the straw is Smerdyakov – number seven. That makes the whole Karamazov crew.' So they get loaves for seven men and despite the stench the dead divvy up their bread with the living."

On the way to the warehouse they passed eight dead Russians on the ground, set in a square, one on top of the other, each head resting on the ankles of the adjacent corpse like the logs of a cabin.

When they got back at noon, they found the warehouse was dark, the guards having put tarp over the windows in anticipation of a possible raid that day.

There was a long line of POWs in front of the john and Timmons, on his way to join them in the dark, stepped on a GI, who cursed him. He realized again how packed the warehouse was. There were no passageways and he had to crawl part of the way on all fours, feeling his way through the straw like an animal until he lost his sense of direction. He clamped his legs together but the tea had done its work. He was losing control. In one of the dark sections he felt about until he located a clear space and quickly took a dump in the straw, praying nobody heard him.

When it was Richard's turn he realized he had no toilet paper. He'd used up his license, ID card, library permit and address book. All he could find in his wallet was Gloria's faded photo. Even in daylight her face had been smudged beyond recognition by the damp. He couldn't visualize the flowing blonde hair, the legs striding up the beach. Without his glasses he could hardly see her at all. It was his only memento, a key to his dreams. But there was no paper and the straw was unthinkable. So, reluctant and bitter, he used the picture.

Then he began to swim over the piled bodies, not knowing where he was heading. He didn't have the strength to keep going, so he rested in an empty spot.

When he returned to his bunk, a siren came on in a steady high whine and the GIs were silent – many lighting up cigarettes to ease their nerves.

"That's the hundred-mile warning," Nutzel said to Timmons. "The B-17s are coming."

"They know we're next to the *stalag*, don't they?" Timmons said.

"We thought we were safe. But they blew up the hospital. And it had a big red cross right on the roof."

"I flew in a B-17," a GI said. "You can't see a thing from up there."

"They have instruments," Timmons said. "They're so anxious to get back to their English pussy they'll drop their load anywhere."

"We're on the main supply route for the Germans," Nutzel said, "The best thing to do when the planes come over is pray."

The door to the front office opened and the Captain came out – still immaculate, his face shaved and powdered, his wavy hair brushed back.

"Captain," Richard said, coming up to the front. "I'm Richard, from I company."

"I hardly recognize you. You look like a pig."

"Have you sent out a message that the hospital was bombed?"

"I'm like you – I just arrived. But they don't trust messages from here. They think that the Germans are sending out propaganda through us."

"Have you formed an escape committee?"

"That's what you prisoners always ask. You think we're in some kind of movie. The officers at the *stalag* have orders from London to discourage anyone from escaping."

Timmons came to join Richard. Turning to the officer he asked, "Why are you so bitchy?"

"I'm tired of your questions."

"Like why you hid at the front and never came up on the line?"

"You don't know everything, smart guy."

When the officer went back to his office Timmons turned to a GI near him, "That was my Captain. He got us caught."

"He's ass-kissing the Germans. And, by the way, are you the guy who's too fucking proud to use the shit can?"

The rumbling of the planes coming over the outskirts of the town interrupted them. They heard Nutzel singing from his bunk, "Ezekiel saw a wheel way up in the middle of the air." The roar of the planes went on and the bombs came down like horses banging their way across a metal roof. These were their planes, Timmons thought, which could squash them with their giant metallic treads.

He gritted his teeth and slid under a bunk for security like he had done as a child when he hid under his bed in a storm. Another blast shook the building and he gripped the beam under the bed, feeling like an ant under a giant foot. Another blast made him shake but it was antiaircraft fire from the town. He waited in terror but it was quiet except for the buzzing of the planes. A spasm of fear pinched his stomach and he prayed he wouldn't lose control again. He crawled out from under the bunk and moved to the window where the tarp had been pulled aside.

A long line of planes were driving across the sky, making the ominous steady buzzing, with patterned white trails stretching behind them, like an artist's dream-like painting of a raid. Richard was proud of the bombers that would end the war, bombing the factories and especially those plants where they were working on the new rockets. But Timmons was petrified by the sound overhead and stared, transfixed, as a single trail of white came down from the lead plane.

Turning, he saw a young nurse following the English medic to the door, holding a box of supplies. He observed the slender blonde with two long braids. For a second he forgot the angry planes overhead and wondered how the medic had corralled the attractive German assistant.

A crackling blast shook the air – the loudest noise he'd ever heard, worse than the tearing of the air by 88 shells. He saw the fear in the nurse's face before he experienced his own. Her face flushed; she dropped her supplies and ran screaming to the door.

A second bomb struck outside, making his ears ring and he hurled himself to the floor.

The GIs were quiet, paralyzed. Only Nutzel intoned, "Ezekiel saw a wheel, way up in the middle of the air." There was another shattering blast that silenced his song; this time the building swayed and the glass from the window near Timmons blew in, spraying pieces on him.

The planes moved off and the buzzing died down, finally fading away.

"Our pilots are our enemy now," Timmons said.

"They don't know we're here," Richard said.

It was a while before they cleared their mind of the new danger and settled back to rest in their bunks.

That night Timmons lay back and had a dream about Jennifer, who led him into her bedroom, helped him off with his clothes and drew him down beside her on the bed, pulling his head down, kissing him with a flick of her tongue, like a hummingbird's wing. She accepted his caresses of her breasts, her smooth neck and flowing hair.

Richard, unable to sleep, reviewed all that had happened to him. He wanted to understand what had taken place; he must straighten it all out before the memories sank into the past; like the figures at the front sinking into the water below the surface of the snow.

10

A short stocky Frenchman who spoke a broken English stopped Richard in the street one morning outside the warehouse. Taking out a small hard dirty loaf of pumpernickel bread he said, "One loaf for a pack of zeegarettes?" Richard still had a pack the army had given him at the front and held it up, saying, "I can get more." The Frenchman smiled as if detecting a bluff but said, "Meet me here later. I'm Dominique."

Richard learned that the French, officially designated allies by the Germans rather than prisoners, were allowed to go into Domburg and make deals for food. Dominique could take a POWs pack into town and get two loaves for it – one for the prisoner and one for himself.

Richard talked to a few non-smokers who'd saved the packs they'd gotten in the past from the Red Cross packages. He told them he'd get a loaf for their cigarettes and convincing them it was a good deal he collected five packs, each containing the usual twenty cigarettes.

In the afternoon, he met Dominique again and impressed him with the five packs. Richard tried to talk him down to sixteen cigarettes for each loaf but the man, making violent gestures, insisted on 20 cigarettes.

Later when Dominique got back from town and gave Richard the loaves for the POWs they talked about their experiences in the war. The Frenchman spoke of his training in the cavalry – how once he rode his horse bareback up and down a field, charging an imaginary tank. One night on patrol he and his horse got lost in a village where a woman told him the Germans had overrun the countryside. Scared witless, he had raced down the back alleys of town, thinking he'd be shot. A German patrol picked him up and, assuming he was a spy, sent him to Domburg as a POW.

Richard felt sorry for him – cut off from home for so many years, deprived of his rights as a man, hustling cigarettes in a foreign town, trying to put food in his mouth and stay alive under the rain of American bombs.

Richard asked him if he'd ever tried to escape and he said some of his friends had broken out and got as far as Belgium before they were caught. The Germans hung four of them. Maybe, he said, they could escape when the Americans got to the Rhine, and the German forces would be in retreat. Richard said he'd like to go with them, and the Frenchman replied that if he could find out when the American Army was coming, they might let him break out with them. He should check with the *stalag* which had short wave radios connecting them to the invasion headquarters in London.

Timmons along with Nutzel was doing some trading with the pack he still had from the front. He met a pug-nosed, brown skinned prisoner with a blackened beard, wearing a toga of dirty sheets that hung down his shoulders, who held out a dark loaf from beneath his filthy garb.

"Twenty," he said to Timmons.

"Sixteen," Timmons said, taking out a rumpled pack from his pocket. Other POWs went through their clothes for objects to trade, bringing out cigarette cases of hammered aluminum, rusty cigarette lighters, pouch bags to hold tobacco. They were chattering like dusty beggars, quoting cigarette prices, their eyes popping out like birds when they saw Timmons' pack.

"They don't get many cigarettes," Nutzel said.

The pug-nosed bargainer lifted up his loaf. "Twenty," he said.

"Sixteen," Timmons insisted.

"Eighteen."

There was a parley among the prisoners, eyeing Timmons. The man in the toga nodded agreement and Timmons, taking eighteen cigarettes from his pack, moved up to the fence. The Italian pushed his left hand with the bread through the wire, his right hand out for the cigarettes. Timmons had his right hand out for the loaf, keeping his left with the butts from the man's grip.

"It's a game of chicken," Nutzel said.

With his cigarettes held back, Timmons slowly pushed his right hand close to the outstretched hand with the bread. The man was pushing the loaf through the enclosure and Timmons tried to grasp it, opening his left hand with the cigarettes for the exchange. Suddenly he let out a cry and lifted his left hand up to his chest – the man had scraped his hand clean of cigarettes, clawing him with his nails while withdrawing his bread back into the compound. The cigarettes had slipped and were mangled inside the yard and the ragged crew snatched like chickens for the feed of broken butts and shreds of paper.

"Pig!" Timmons shouted, his hand streaked with blood and tobacco.

"You lost," Nutzel said.

Depressed, Timmons went back into the warehouse, arriving just as the hundred-mile steady siren came on from the town and soon he heard the flying fortresses buzzing.

The tarp for darkening the room didn't fully cover a few windows and there was some light in the room. The men were unusually silent and despite the Captain's warning, the smokers who still had butts lit up.

Nutzel saw Timmons, morbid and scared in his bunk, opening and shutting a matchbox.

"What's in the box?" Nutzel asked him.

"None of your business," Timmons said.

Nutzel leaned into Timmons' bunk and ripped the matchbox out of his hands and held it up. "I got it," he shouted. "I got the magic box. What are you hiding?"

"Give me that, you creep," Timmons said.

"Look what I got," Nutzel said, holding up the matchbox and sliding open the small drawer. "It's hair all squished up."

"Let me have it," Timmons said, going for the box.

"Now listen, everybody, according to the note in the box, it contains the immortal cunt hair of Timmons' English whore."

The GIs roared with laughter. To get his box, Timmons dove for Nutzel's legs, wrestled him into the straw and finally turned him over. Taking his legs he pushed him across the floor like a wheelbarrow. When Nutzel was out of breath, his mouth full of straw, Timmons slapped him on the back and let him go. The box had fallen out of Nutzel's hand in the struggle and the prized hair had spilled into the straw.

"You shouldn't make fun of me," Timmons said.

"Don't let them get you down, buddy," Richard said.

The planes were now directly over the warehouse, ending the discord. A bomb landed in the railroad yard; another exploded outside Timmons' window, shaking the building. The planes passed on but the men still remained quiet.

Richard went outside to escape the confinement of the warehouse. He must get information to Dominique he thought and break out of this hell hole.

One of the POWs had an Air Corps sheepskin jacket which he'd inherited from a dead buddy in the camp. Dominique had seen the jacket and meeting Richard in the street, asked him if the owner might trade it for bread – for three loaves.

Richard, who wanted to please the Frenchman for future deals, got the prisoner to agree to the exchange and turned the jacket over to a delighted Dominique in return for the loaves.

One morning the Captain called Timmons into his office, where he felt the sudden blast of heat from the potbellied stove.

"You live well," Timmons said.

"I didn't ask you in to discuss how I live," the Captain said. "I want you to stop wheeling and dealing for cigarettes. The guards don't like it."

"It's our only chance to get bread."

"The Germans cut our rations because of the bombings. They're getting mean. They won't let the English medic come anymore to check the men. The raids are going to get worse, now that our army's across the Roer River."

Timmons was excited by the news but asked, "Where do you get your food, Captain?"

"I eat what everyone else eats."

"Did the Germans offer you a deal to stay with the enlisted men – good clothes, a fire, food?"

"I won't dignify that with a reply."

"Why don't we get any Red Cross food parcels?"

"The supply lines are cut off."

"They say there are hundreds of parcels somewhere. Nutzel got prunes from a guy at the *stalag*. They could only come from a Red Cross package."

"There used to be food parcels here."

"Captain, have you sent out word by short wave that we're at this warehouse?"

"As I told you, the Allies think our short-wave messages are sent out on orders from the Germans, to keep our planes off the supply lines."

"What's the Geneva Convention say about housing prisoners in a railroad yard?"

"The Germans say they don't have any place for us, with so many prisoners coming in from Belgium."

"Why do you pretend you don't know us?"

"I can't show preferential treatment to anybody."

"You don't show anyone preferential treatment. You live for yourself."

Later the Captain called Richard into his office.

"I warned your buddy and now I'm warning you. Stop dealing with the frogs. The guards don't like it. Now you're going to town for your interrogation."

"Did you set that up?"

"It's routine. Everybody goes eventually. You'll get a haircut first."

The barber, a Greek POW with curling slick hair, met Richard at a desk outside the Captain's office, put powder on

116

his face, and with a long dull razor gave him a dry shave that scraped his skin but made him feel clean.

As Richard prepared to go with a guard, the Captain said from his door, "Don't be a wise guy with Herr Todd."

The guard took him out – it was a clear windy day – and they walked into town until they came to the winding streets and decaying timber-crossed houses of old Domburg. They stopped at a school building with a sign *Oberschule* over the door, its roof half burnt off from the raids.

The guard led him into a cold anteroom of the schoolhouse and Richard was restless, feeling the bubbling ache in his chest again. After an hour or so the guard took him into a small bathroom with individual cubicles and rubber tubing hanging down from the wall. He was told to remove his clothes and take a shower. He stripped and, shaking from the cold, got in the tub behind the curtain. There he picked up a shower head with a long tube and the guard reached his hand in and turned on the icy water. Richard let it roll over his head, body, neck and groin. He sprayed his foot which was no longer painful and tried to keep the water off his chest which was sensitive to any pressure. He found a piece of soap on the ledge but couldn't work up a lather with it. The hand reached in and turned the water off, giving him a small rag to dry himself. He had trouble getting his stiff long-johns on, realizing that filth had become part of his life. His shirt was gone and he put his pants on, feeling his chest throb from his wet bandages.

The guard took him to an office where the interrogator sat, dressed and bundled up against the cold, a toad of a man with bent silver glasses and a military cross on his lapel. He was sucking on a pipe and blowing clouds of smoke into the air towards Richard. The guard left and the interrogator, his wrist and finger shaking from an infirmity, waved Richard to a low chair. Checking a pad on his desk he said, "Private Richard Glasgow, right?"

"Yes. 12109170," he replied, shivering.

"They're delousing your shirt."

Planes droned overhead, which surprised Richard. He hadn't heard the hundred-mile warning. The interrogator went to the window, looking up as the buzzing increased. He pulled the black curtain down and leaned over Richard's chair, blowing smoke at him, which made his eyes smart. "Did you come through Ehrenbreitstein where the two rivers meet?"

Richard recalled the destruction on both sides of the Rhine – shattered blocks of houses, rooms open to the sky, street signs twisted like candy canes. He wondered if he could get some information. "You mean where the Americans crossed the Rhine?"

"No, they're not across the Rhine. Is that where you were captured?"

"I can't tell you."

"You can only tell me your name, rank, and serial number. Otherwise you could tell me what you learned in college; you could explain the theory of relativity to me." He began to laugh and, when he stopped, picked up a glass from the table and drank the entire contents. Richard figured he had already downed a few glasses of schnapps.

A bomb landed a few streets away and the interrogator's hand shook though he looked Richard right in the eye. "We can take anything you gangsters drop on us. You hit the Cologne cathedral with hundreds of bombs. But all you did was uncover a jewel – an ancient statue of Bacchus riding on a satyr." There was a put-putting sound like a motorcycle warming up and the man went to the window, pulled the blind halfway up. A long cigar-shaped rocket buzzed across the sky like the ones Richard had seen over London.

"You see that? It's our new weapon and there are thousands like it. When it gets to England it will blow up a city block. We will soon make a bomb the size of a pineapple that will wipe out London and New York."

Richard wondered if he was talking about the atom bomb. He remembered seeing Einstein once in college – short, stocky, wide-eyed, in baggy pants, with strands of hair falling around

118

his ears like a mop. Richard had asked him a question at the lecture when everyone else was too awed to say a word. "Should we develop an atom bomb?" he had asked. And the great man laughed with a spasm, his hair shaking as if his body wasn't obeying the commands from his head. "Eh, weh," he said. "If Hitler gets the bomb first, he could blow everybody up." His shoulders had shaken and Richard had stared at the scientist whose laugh echoed through the halls, one burst after another like a chain reaction.

The interrogator leaned over and blew puffs of smoke into his face, interrupting his reverie. "Here in Domburg, Herr Glasgow," he said, "you will be buried by your own planes."

He laughed until he choked and had to take the pipe out of his mouth. When he regained his composure he came over to Richard and pinched his arm. "The Captain tells me you're a smart boy and like to trade cigarettes for bread. You're a friend of Dominique's, is that right?" Getting no reply, the man leaned over and pinched Richard's nipple, making him wince.

"What are you thinking about, Good Soldier Schweik?" Again he pinched his nipple. "You buy cigarettes and then what? You want to break out of the warehouse like some prisoners did last year? Come on, talk to me. And what's wrong with your eyes? You're blinking all the time."

"I lost my glasses."

"If you come talk to me – tell me what GIs you bargain with – I'll get you a new pair. I'll get you a doctor to take care of that scratch on your chest. I'll even get some schnapps to warm you up."

He pinched him above the chest bandage and Richard shook with pain. "What's wrong with you?" The man's eyebrows went up and down like shutters. "You don't want to talk to me. You're a hero. You only give your name, rank, and serial number. But let me tell you – if you try to break out with the French I'll lock you up in a crypt under the church. The Captain keeps me informed about trouble-makers like you. So watch out." He got up and called the guard, who came in and gave Richard his shirt.

On the road back Richard felt the strong wind rip into him, triggering a chest pain. The Captain stopped him on his way into the warehouse as if he'd been waiting for him. "How did it go?" he asked.

"I gave him my name, rank, and serial number."

"Did he warn you about the French?"

"He said you had talked to him about me."

"I have to keep the Germans happy so they treat us right. I have to think of everyone in this warehouse."

"He wanted me to rat on the others the way you're doing."

"Don't be a smart-ass. And keep away from the French, or you'll be on my shit list."

Lying back in his bunk that night, Timmons felt depressed. His time was passing, his life drifting away, as a neighbor's barn had once floated off during a flood. Later he heard someone come in and look through the straw next to him for a place to settle. "Anybody awake?" the new arrival asked.

"Yeah," Timmons said. "You just come in?"

"Right. I got caught at the river."

"Which river?"

"The Rhine. I was one of the first to sneak across the Remagen Bridge. But all our guys have now crossed over the river."

Timmons shouted, "Yahooooooooo," waking the sleepers. And he yelled over at Richard, "Yes, yes. We're going to get out of here."

11

The next morning Dominique welcomed Richard with a grin and a handshake, sporting his new jacket with the full white fur collar.

"I've got news for you," Richard said.

"Good. Come with me," the Frenchman replied. He took Richard by the arm and led him through an opening in the wire at the south end of the compound, where they entered a block-long former hospital with the sign *Krankenhaus* over the door. Inside the main room Frenchmen were seated at a long table with red cloth and metal plates full of sausages and potatoes. They were enjoying a bowl of thick bean soup with hunks of pumpernickel bread. A sweet-smelling cereal like cream of wheat was heating on the stove. They didn't interrupt their banquet to take note of Richard who figured they didn't speak English.

"What news?" the Frenchman asked, as they sat down.

"What's it worth?" Richard said with a smile.

"You can join us in the shelters when the bombers come over."

"You said you had plans to get out."

"We have to know when the American Army will come."

"If I tell you can my friend and I join you in the breakout?"

"I think so." There was a grumbling from the seated diners who had an inkling of what Dominique was agreeing to but he waved them to be quiet.

"The 9th Armored crossed the Rhine at Remagen Bridge," Richard said.

"How do you know?" Dominique asked.

"A GI came into the warehouse from the 9th. He was the first across the bridge. He said the east bank is under Allied control from Remagen to Koblenz and south to Mainz."

"It might be a good time for a boat ride," the Frenchman said.

He set down the terms for the breakout. They first had to

check his information that the Rhine was safe from Remagen to Koblenz. They would leave in a couple of days, a few hours before the noon raid. Richard and his friend would put on French uniforms he'd get for them. They were scheduled to work at the graveyard, burying the dead. After the burials they would return by way of the cathedral, arriving just about the time of the noon raid. Often the guards went into their shelter during the raids and made them stand outside on the church steps. With luck when the planes came over they could run into the woods behind the church. Then they would head for the river by way of the camp for political prisoners. He showed Richard the route on the map, how they would come to the river Lahn. At an arranged spot some French friends would have a boat tied up for them. At night they would row the boat southwest along the curving river to Bad Ems. There, they would ditch the boat and walk towards Koblenz to make contact with the American forces. They must avoid retreating Germans and watch out for the fire from the advancing GIs.

Richard agreed to the plan. To seal the bargain Dominique gave him a cake of the prized Kernseife soap, telling him that the people of Domburg didn't even have that kind of soap. He got it from the GIs at the *stalag*. He said that if there was a dollar in it the Americans could come up with anything. There was even talk that the U.S. supplied the pellets used to gas political prisoners. Richard said it sounded like a rumor. Dominique asked him why so many Americans were mistreated in the warehouse and why Richard wasn't at the *stalag*. He replied that there wasn't any room at the prison camp. But the man shook his head in disbelief.

They agreed that on the day chosen for the breakout they would meet at noon at the French compound.

Back at his bunk Timmons was restless. He resented the coming of the preacher from the *stalag* despite the report that the evangelist had gifts for the POWs.

He was frying potatoes on the stove, complaining that he didn't have any fat, and the silver-colored metal from the pan had come off on the spuds. He looked over at Richard, his cheeks sunk in from hunger, his jacket torn and covered with leopard spots of black grease. To keep calm during the bombing he read and read without his glasses – the book held close to his face – and his eyes had blood spots. Often he kept them closed to rest them. When he maneuvered down the aisle of the darkened room he seemed to be walking in his sleep.

A sudden explosion shook the building, jolting them. Timmons looked out of one uncovered window and saw smoke pouring out of the German headquarters next to the station.

"What's happening?" he asked Richard.

"There must be some small planes – P-51s maybe – bombing the town. But they probably know we're here in the warehouse."

"They don't know we're here. And they'll keep bombing us. We'll probably catch it from both sides now."

"It's the only way we can get out. The war's almost over."

"That's great – if we survive."

A tip-off of their coming release was the behavior of Dewey who had just brought in a huge can of tea. To curry their favor, bending low like an obsequious waiter, he served the tea to his American prisoners with an ingratiating smile. Richard figured the guard knew his army was being chased across the Fatherland and soon he'd be a prisoner himself – turn in his greatcoat and pretty chevrons for a soggy pair of POW overalls.

Timmons stood by the window and enjoyed his morning hot tea while Richard sat on the edge of his bunk, reading a book.

"How can you read at a time like this?" Timmons asked.

"It's the only thing that keeps me going."

In the early afternoon the Captain came out of his office, walking easily now, his foot seemingly healed. "Attention!" he shouted and the men were startled, grumbling at the surprise of the command. "I can tell you, my friends, that the Germans will fight for every bloody street and our pilots are going to blast away at us. We expect a massive raid today, so no lights, no smoking. And don't pull off the cardboard from the windows, however dark it is. The war's coming to an end, so this may be my last word to you." There was a mocking cheer from the POWs. "You may howl. But there are some things you don't understand."

"Yeah," Timmons said, "like how you always keep so fat and sassy. What about our food parcels? Where did you hide them?"

"I never saw any food parcels," the Captain said, going back to his office where he turned and said, "One final word – I want you to pay attention to Brother Bob. He's come all the way from the *stalag* to talk to you. So listen – it'll be good for your souls."

"Hello, men," a voice called out from the door. The evangelist stood in the light that came through a slot in the window covering – a handsome, ruddy man in an immaculate OD uniform, his face shaven close and powdered like the Captain's. "I welcome you in the name of the Lord," he said in a clipped voice, as if he were practicing his diction.

"Give us your blessing, Brother Bob," Nutzel said.

"We gather together in His name," the preacher went on. "He knows you are anxious to see your loved ones again, who are praying for you. You're all experiencing deprivation. When I was going with my fiancée I remember long periods of separation."

"It must've been pretty hard for you," someone said. Richard realized it was the custom to razz the preacher, who responded with a smile.

"My friends," the preacher said. "I've come here today to put on a play that I've adapted."

A small group of POWs squatted in front of the preacher, anxious for a diversion.

"I need three actors to read the parts. Any volunteers?"

Richard raised his hand, saying, "If I can read the lines."

"Okay, the preacher said, "you can be the main character, Everyman. Now I need somebody to play Everyman's friend." Richard nodded to Timmons, who reluctantly agreed to take the part. "Finally we need an actor to play Death." Nobody volunteered, until Nutzel finally said "I'll take that role."

"Now here are your parts," the preacher said, handing out a sheet of dialogue to each volunteer. And here's the plot – God has Death tell Everyman he must go on a journey but Everyman doesn't like the idea of a trip with Death. Well, you'll see how it turns out. I'll speak first as the voice of God:

GOD:	I find that here on earth
	There's one who never thanks me
	For all the good
	I've done for him.
	And so I call on Death.
DEATH:	What can I do for you?
GOD:	Death, go to Everyman
	And tell him he must go
	On a pilgrimage with you.
DEATH:	I'll tell him what you wish
	And here he comes.
	"Oh, Everyman, stop there,
	God has a word for you."
EVERYMAN:	What does He want?
DEATH:	He wants you to go with me
	On a pilgrimage.
EVERYMAN:	But I'm not ready for a trip.
DEATH:	Yet you must go.
EVERYMAN:	Can someone go with me?
DEATH:	Yes, you can take a friend
	If one will make the trip with you.
EVERYMAN:	Here comes my friend –
	I know he'll back me up.

	"Dear friend, I have to go
	On a fateful journey,
	And need a friend to go with me."
FRIEND:	I'll go with you,
	And when will we return?
EVERYMAN:	We never will return.
FRIEND:	Who told you this?
EVERYMAN:	That fellow, Death.
FRIEND:	My God, if it was Death
	Who told you this,
	I cannot go with you
	On such a trip.
	Good-bye my friend,
	You'll have to go alone.
GOD:	I say to all the faithful now
	This Everyman, I know,
	Adored my Son –
	So when you all meet Death
	And find you die alone –
	Remember Everyman
	Who dying followed Christ,
	So I forgave his sins
	And now he's crowned on high
	Where he can hear
	Among the hosts
	The Choir of angels sing.

The POWs who listened attentively during the reading remained silent at the end.

"What a boring scene," Timmons said.

"It's an old morality play," Richard said.

The preacher went on, "Now if anyone will accept Jesus like Everyman I have a prize for them, donated by the POWs at the *stalag*. Those who come forward and accept Jesus will get a brand new roll of toilet paper. Who will be first?"

The GIs rushed to the front, pushing each other and cursing. Richard wondered if he was just being stupid not getting into the line. What would he do if he had a new stomach spasm that he couldn't control in the dark? He saw Timmons hesitate to join the line.

"Come and accept Jesus," the preacher intoned. The POWs in the line approached the evangelist who gave each of them a new roll. Timmons slipped into the line but when he got to Brother Bob the last roll had been handed out.

"What a crock," he said to Richard. "You have to accept Jesus to get shit paper."

There was the hum of approaching planes.

"I know we're in the dark," the preacher said, "but you can hear my voice. It's going to be tough for you in the next few hours. But men are suffering everywhere and none will suffer more than He did for us."

"Hallelujah," Nutzel said.

The hum of the planes began, scaring the POWs because there had been no warning siren. Through a small uncovered hole in the window Timmons saw the fortresses coming. "If we accept Him," Timmons shouted at the evangelist, "will they stop bombing us?"

"The more they bomb the Germans the sooner we'll get out," the preacher said, smiling, as if the drone of the planes was music accompanying him. "We're all afraid of death. But just as you will toss off these rags when you get out, so you will cast off this body when you're free of this life."

A blast of antiaircraft sounded from the town and Timmons saw the small grey puffs of flak dotting the sky. A military truck drove across a field, forcing a man and his wagon of lumber into a ditch.

The guard Dewey ran behind the cement shelter on the side of a still-smoking German headquarters.

"Who will accept Jesus?" the preacher said.

"I do," Nutzel said.

More antiaircraft raked the sky.

"Speak to us, Brother Bob," Nutzel said.

"If any of you have sins on your heart, now is the time to confess," the man went on.

"I'm not confessing anything," Timmons said.

"You may be the worst sinner," Nutzel said.

"Who will accept Jesus?" the preacher asked.

"You're all scared," Timmons said. "After the raid you'll go right back to lying and stealing."

"Brother Bob," Nutzel said, "ask the Lord to help us."

"Yeah," Timmons said, "God is going to ask those pilots to drop their bombs on every motherfucker except you."

"This is no time for blasphemy," Nutzel said. "We'll all suffer for your foul mouth."

The planes roared overhead as if to punctuate his warning.

"Yeah, lay off the dirty talk," someone said.

"Why?" Timmons said. "Just because you're pissing in your pants?"

The planes buzzed with a new menacing sound. The POWs were silenced, expecting real danger. Would the planes never pass on? Timmons thought.

"Our Father who art in heaven," the preacher began, "hallowed be Thy name."

The fortresses sounded like they were a few feet above the roof and the bombs came whistling down.

"Confess," the preacher said. "Come to Jesus. Accept Him while there's time."

"What the hell are you babbling about?" Timmons shouted.

There was a shattering blast and through the uncovered window Timmons had a glimpse of the town, as in the lens of a camera. The towers of the small church folded up, its windows gouged out. He heard the furious banging rattle of bombs coming down onto the railroad yard.

Nothing before had given Timmons such a sense of his own approaching death, coming haphazardly at him from the sky. He could foresee his own burial and suffocation under the debris. A frightened POW with the same presentiment leapt off his bed and hit him on the way down. Timmons looked at Richard as if to say, "This is it," and a bomb exploded on the tracks outside, making the men lie still.

Another blast rocked the building and Richard felt his lungs collapse under enormous pressure as if a doctor was testing his chest with a downward motion of two powerful arms. The timber above was spinning down and the POWs fell through the boards as the floor went out from underneath and the walls closed around them like a box folding. Richard felt a blow on his neck and his mouth filled with plaster. Gagging, he fell deeper into a new hole opening up into the cellar, and he couldn't budge. As he stuck a foot out of the hole, wood crashed in on him and he yanked his foot back. He had been hit in a reclining position and spun around so he was upside down, pressed against a beam, his back framed by wooden planks. His arms were fastened to his sides and his legs were buried in dust and straw like a hastily made grave.

"Timmons?" he called out.

"Yes," his friend said, below him.

It seemed like years before a GI stepped on Richard's sore foot, dug around it and finally cleared away the timber and bed-boards folded around his body and lifted him out. Richard felt his limbs and figured he hadn't broken any bones. He checked the cuts on his nose, lips, arms and legs, daubing the bleeding skin with a piece of his torn shirt. There seemed to be no further injury to his chest.

"Timmons," he said, "are you okay?"

"Here," he said, deep inside the cavity. Richard clawed away at the wood and plaster and with the help of the GI cleared a passage into the depths of the basement. They had to remove the pile of debris before they finally eased Timmons out - a clown with a powdered face, his clothes half ripped off, his bloodshot eyes filled with dust.

They both waded through the broken beds and fallen posts to look for others but it was oddly silent, as if they had come upon a ruin long after some catastrophe. Timmons stumbled into a hole and stepped on a body.

They cleared away more debris and unearthed a white mummified corpse and recognized Nutzel's dirty swathed head bandage and Air Corps insignia. He was stretched out as in a morgue, his mouth wide open, tongue and beard colored with plaster. He wasn't breathing and there was a deep red channel of a cut running down his neck, with a jagged piece of wood sticking out of his throat.

Stumbling to the surface over the rocks and debris, Timmons met a guard who motioned for them to climb out of the wreckage and line up with those who could still walk.

Would there be no end to this meaningless destruction of their warehouse? The bombings of course would increase as the American forces closed in on the last German defenses.

He wondered if even Richard, stumbling away from the scattered rocks and wooden planks of the building, still thought everything made sense.

12

The following day, the guards rounded up the prisoners from the ruined warehouse and took them to a nearby deserted barn where they settled on the straw-covered floor.

During the night, before turning in, Timmons said to Richard, "What in hell is going on? We've never changed our clothes. We haven't had a bath in six months. We don't have any shit paper. We stink to high heaven."

"Germany's in a state of collapse. POWs used to have food parcels, a library and a concert on Saturday night. The British prisoners took courses by mail from Oxford."

"How does that affect us?"

"We became prisoners at the wrong time."

"But, Richard, how did we get into this mess?"

"Well, we volunteered to come here. Others stayed at home, claiming exemption for bad eyes or a heart murmur or because they peed in their beds. At least we showed some hair in agreeing to serve."

"But we came with a totally fucked-up outfit. We got a Captain who was afraid of his shadow."

"In peacetime good men never joined the army. So we ended up with officers like Plankton."

"That doesn't help us much."

"It should help you understand what happened."

"None of our officers knew what was going on at the front. And we had no artillery – the ammo never arrived."

"Things like that happen in wartime."

"And we ended up in a crossfire, shooting at our own guys."

"That's because of the snow and fog. They couldn't see us and we couldn't see them."

"There you go – trying to make sense out of it. Our division was defeated, wiped out in a few weeks."

"*We* never confronted the enemy. The Captain forced us at gunpoint to surrender to the Germans. Therefore, you and I were not defeated."

"Then our pilots bombed the POW camp and buried us."

"They can't see what they're bombing at that height."

"So they're useless."

"They do their best."

"Richard, why can't you see how ridiculous everything is?"

"Sometimes in a war, things don't work out as we'd like. Timmons, you have to read *The Iliad*. Homer says that in battle the gods will take one side or the other, for no particular reason. War doesn't go according to some plan."

"It should make sense."

"You're looking at it from the wrong end of the telescope."

"And I think you're looking at it from the rosey side. But, Richard, maybe you're right. You know more than I do. You've read the right books. Here I am – I just finished this novel, *Hungry Thighs*, a cheap sex tale. I enjoyed it. I've never read the kind of books you like. I didn't go to college. I just worked as a gardener – digging in the ground, planting bushes, spreading compost to make things grow. I'm ignorant of most everything else. You know a lot."

"Who cares if you didn't go to college? You know how things work. Everything I know I got out of books."

"Well, what have you learned? What does anything mean? Is there any point to life at all?"

"I think there is."

"Is there a God?"

"I have to think so."

"Then why does He allow women and children to die of disease? Why does He let half the planet starve?"

"We don't know exactly why. I heard Einstein give a talk once in college and he said Spinoza was right. God's not a person. We may love Him but He doesn't love us."

"So He doesn't give a damn about us."

"Einstein said that God's too busy keeping the planets in position – organizing space."

"You actually heard Einstein?"

"I once saw him walking up and down in front of my dorm.

He seemed to be dreaming. Then he suddenly turned and walked in another direction. I had the wild idea that I might actually be seeing him when he got the final unified theory, explaining everything – like seeing Newton when the apple fell. But he probably just had to go to the john."

"What did he believe?"

"He believed in the mystery of the world. And the miracle, he said, is that we can comprehend that mystery. What happens does not occur by accident, he thought. God does not play dice with the universe."

"But everything that happened to us happened by accident."

"That's because men screwed up."

"But how can anyone believe in a God?"

"Some scientist said, and I remember his exact words – if after the big bang, the rate of expansion had been smaller by even one part in a hundred thousand million million, the universe would have collapsed. If the expansion rate at one second had been larger by the same amount, the universe would've ended up empty. The creator must've known that the expansion had to be exactly that rate or we wouldn't be here. The scientist said, when we figure out the theory of everything, we'll know the mind of God."

"When will we know everything?"

"Maybe centuries from now."

"What good will that do us? We'll be gone."

"We'll have added our bit of knowledge toward the final answer."

"Were we adding to that knowledge by squatting in a ditch waiting to shoot a German or get shot by one?"

"If Hitler wins, there won't be much hope of discovering anything in the future. I don't know exactly what we're doing, but we have to believe there's a reason for what we've done. But, Timmy, let's look on the bright side. Didn't you have fun in England?"

"I'll never forget those English girls. They were so friendly. Once I paid the thirty bucks they did anything I asked them to do – even crazy things – switching positions, the three of them rolling around on all sides of me, taking turns kissing me, letting me take them one at a time, laughing, making it all seem perfectly normal. Afterward, when I was all tired out, they gave me a hot bath. Jennifer wanted me to look her up after the war – if we ever get back. That's what I'm living for."

"I'll never forget I saw Shakespeare's home. And I walked the streets of London. I saw Westminster Abbey where the great poets are buried. And I met the poet, Eliot, who was kind enough to read his new poem to me. Gloria will be amazed when she hears that all this happened to me. So let's sleep, Timmy, and dream about the good things."

13

A corner of the warehouse was still smoldering in the morning and the prisoners looked out from their new home in the barn and saw a hill of blown-up, small cardboard boxes and the garbage ejected from them: crushed silver tins of oozing sardines; small broken jelly jars drowned in marmalade; peanut butter on the rims of sharp glass; prunes covered with plaster; shreds of tobacco sprinkled everywhere; and the white milk substitute tossed by the wind like raining powder. A sea of garbage. Timmons figured that the mess of food blown out of the warehouse must've been the Red Cross food hidden by the Captain and denied to them. A GI jumped over a wall and picked up a broken jar and licked the dirty jam, cutting his tongue. Another joined him, scraping together some tobacco to make a cigarette. There was little worth scavenging.

Richard figured he must get out of town at all costs.

And then he saw Captain Plankton being led away from the side of the ruined building by two guards.

"What're they doing with him?" Timmons asked.

"I heard a rumor he cheated on his German pals," one of the prisoners said.

"I hope they shoot him," Timmons said.

Dominique emerged from the crowd and came up to Richard and pulling him aside said, "Come with me, you and your friend." As they walked to the French compound he explained that the time had come. They would make a break when the guards took them to bury the dead. It would also be possible to sneak Richard and his friend through the gate with them.

He gave them both a brown French overcoat and calot cap. Dominique and two other Frenchmen walked with them to the sentry post where they picked up their guards. Timmons was restless, trying to merge with his anonymous companions. The two guards, after a cursory check, let them pass through the gate and led them to a country road that had deep holes in it from the raids. The air was warmer and Richard skipped a few feet to exercise his bad foot.

They climbed a small hill at Lindenweg and looked ahead at a narrow avenue of pines. At the top was the grave site, with crosses stuck in at odd angles, a huge collective pit that had been dug by previous work gangs. Tracks had been drawn in the dirt by the trucks that had brought the dead up the hill. Behind the huge pit were the bodies to be buried: three GIs they recognized from the warehouse, and seven Russians from the foreign quarters. To their surprise they saw the corpse of the guard Dewey, his forehead caved in, probably from a blow during the bombing. His body was already rigid like a stone carving.

They were ordered to take shovels and begin digging. Approaching the dead, Timmons thought they looked like football players who might get up and run onto the field. He took the first body by the armpits while Richard lifted the legs. Under their fingers the limbs moved. Timmons, queasy from the morning's rutabaga soup, was afraid he'd get sick. He imagined the GI was alive and they were merely helping him off the playing field. They lowered the body into the grave where it slid sideways into position; they filled in the hole but Timmons couldn't look at the face as he covered it with dirt.

After the POWs and Dewey were buried, the guards led them all to the cathedral road. The timing was good. As they walked up the hill to the church they heard the hundred-mile siren blare out its warning.

They arrived at the squat cathedral with its unmatched spires, which they'd passed on their way into Domburg. One of the stained-glass windows revealed a fat snarling pig with a huge snout, representing one of the seven sins.

Richard, observing the Gothic structure, thought of old Germanic tales he'd read, describing moss-covered chapels and blood-stained tapestries. He smiled, imagining vaults with rows and rows of sculptured skeletons with shiny, toothy grins.

Hearing a noise behind him he turned and saw citizens rushing up the hill as if running for their lives. They passed the

POWs, staring at them with hate and ran to the shelter at the top. The planes were coming over the town.

The French under Dominique's lead were watching the two guards, gauging the right moment to run into the woods under the pretext of avoiding the bombs. The trailing white flares came down from the lead planes in V patterns and Richard, even without his glasses, was spellbound by the hazy beauty of the distant bombs gliding down on the eastern end of town. The guards, who must've been used to such raids, looked calmly toward Domburg, but stood near the shelter for safety.

They all watched the bombs falling as the cluster of planes, in tight formations of twelve each, drove across the sky among white clouds that were mirror images of the bursts from the antiaircraft guns. The bombs were dropping on the town and curving toward them like slanting rain. The first struck around the town hall near the statue of the soldier in the square; others worked their way up the hill like climbers toward the cathedral. Richard looked at Dominique for a sign, afraid of the bombs but anxious to make his break into the woods. The guards sensing the danger to themselves moved with the POWs in the direction of the shelter. A few citizens seeing the POWs coming shouted for them to stay out, *"Heraus, heraus."*

An old man outside the shelter grabbed Timmons by the neck and spun him into the street, crying, *"Heraus, heraus."* The guards, confused by their duty to guard the POWs and yet appease the townspeople, waved the prisoners away from the shelter. A bomb crashed into the side of the cathedral, blowing out the stained glass window with the pig's snout, and the guards, caught by surprise, panicked and ducked into the shelter. Dominique waved his hand and the French took off as if they were running to escape from the hit. More bombs landed around them and they got into the woods just as the raid ended.

The French moved quickly through the trees and Richard and Timmons tried to keep up with them. Dominique slowed his men down to let them catch up and together they came to a hill giving them a view of the valley and the political camp east of the town.

Later they saw a narrow clearing in the woods below and made out a caterpillar line of figures weaving along the tracks. Coming closer they saw men and women with shaved heads like emaciated boys, carrying picks and shovels. Several women were hauling boards, balancing them on their heads and they entered a narrow strip of land between a wire fence and a ditch running around a huge camp – dark robots wearing black-and-white striped pants like movie comics, their shawls in rags, stumbling along in thick wooden shoes.

Passing a stream close to a camp, they saw a barbed wire fence on the other side of the water. A young girl, short, black-skinned, with long black hair appeared behind the wire, in the striped prison trousers, naked to the waist, her head shaven close. Taking advantage of the afternoon sun she was washing her clothes in the dirty stream.

Richard and Timmons stopped, letting the others go ahead of them. Hidden by the trees they stared at the woman with a hollow chest and dark eyes, as if she were sick. Why, they wondered, was she a prisoner? They watched her as she bent over the stream, scrubbing her black-and-white striped shirt and underclothes.

Dominique yelled at them to keep moving but they took a last look at the prisoner. Richard remembered a painting he'd seen of a young awkward woman framed by a flowered bank near a spring. The prisoner was framed by an ugly barbed wire, with the backdrop of a muddy bank and dirty water. Why had she been driven into the cruel woods?

"Who are they?" Timmons asked Dominique.

"Political prisoners. Some are gypsies the Nazis want to exterminate."

"My God," Richard said.

"I wonder why they'd burn them," Timmons said.

They saw hundreds in the camp, lining up to be counted. A cloud of black smoke blew over the entire area. They smelled a weird sweet odor.

"The stink is bad, eh?" Dominique said. He told them how he had once driven a truck down the wrong road, carrying a load of civilians killed in the raids. He ended up in that camp below and saw the black cloud, thinking they were burning debris or dead animals. The smell had made him sick. It was dark and on the way out he passed a German guard. Sticking his head out of the truck he asked the German what the stench was. The German thought he was a guard and mentioned Blaugas. They were doing away with political prisoners. Richard said he had heard they burned the German bodies to prevent infection but Dominique said he had taken the civilian bodies to another grave. In the political camp down there they were gassing their own people and burning them.

Richard felt he'd never forget the young, gaunt gypsy girl framed by the barbed wire, who was destined to be burnt. He had the lines of a poem forming in his head, to remind himself of the horror.

They took a path toward the river Lahn and midway they had a clear view of Domburg. To the east they saw a tank wiggling through a cut in the distant hill, tossing up clouds of dust. To their surprise a second tank came up behind the first, and then a third. Each machine rose up and then leveled out on the road. The first one opened fire at the town with a deafening roar, its smoke drifting up in the clear air. They obviously weren't German tanks firing on the town.

"They look like Americans," Timmons said. "Let's get closer." Dominique reversed their direction so they were moving back toward the town. They saw the second tank blast away and the third echoed its roar. Small arms fire came from the *stalag* area around the sentry towers. The first tank turned in the direction of the tower and fired a shell that exploded next to the *stalag*. The second tank fired and carved a hole in the autobahn like a tear in a pool table. Timmons could hardly keep from shouting. They might soon be free.

He heard popgun noises coming from Domburg and saw people crawling back and forth on the roofs in the town, firing rifles at the tanks. The shooting continued and again the tanks answered with shells that churned up the hill not far from the warehouse. The people on the roofs fired away, the tanks shot back, and two of the houses near the prison camp collapsed. They saw prisoners racing from the *stalag* toward the tanks – a mad rush of ants. Many of them got to the tanks and climbed on for a ride to freedom.

"Let's join them," Timmons shouted. "It's over. We're out. Yahoooooo!" The Frenchman smiled and started down the hill that would lead to the road back to town. Shells landed near the tanks and there was a blast of continuous sound from the east, but it was impossible to tell the source.

To Timmons' amazement the tanks turned with their cargo of POWs and headed away from Domburg. The roof fighters popped away as if they'd won the battle against the tanks, which had driven onto the autobahn and were heading in Timmons' direction. He couldn't believe the Americans were retreating. He led the Frenchmen down the hill toward the approaching tanks, which were loaded with GIs.

When he came up to the first one, he found the POWs clustered together on the machine, in a state of panic. He walked up to a GI who was trying to keep his place on the back of the tank.

"What's happening?" he asked.

"We're cut off," the GI said.

"Why is the army going back?"

"This isn't the army. It's a suicide outfit sent to liberate our camp. But the Germans closed in on them."

They learned that the GI had burnt down their *stalag* quarters, thinking they were being freed by Patton, who had sent a small raiding force into the region to free the prisoners. But it had turned into a rout. Some of Patton's men, along with a group of POWs racing out of the *stalag*, had been mowed down.

Small arms fire came at them from all directions; machine gun bullets whipped into the scattering lines, hitting several of the GIs nestled on the American tanks. Several POWs scrambled off the tank and headed for the woods, but a rapping of machine gun fire cut down four or five of the leaders of the mad rush.

There was an enormous explosion and the tank with a few POWs clinging to it blew up. A blast came from an artillery gun in the woods and the second American tank went up in flames, its crew leaping out and joining the POWs in the race for the trees. Artillery fire could be heard from the surrounding hills and the shells began whining overhead and falling around the retreating Americans. Machine guns raked the area until everyone was down: some killed, others injured and screaming, huddled beside the ruined tanks.

The entire region from the valley up to the northern hills was alive with enemy soldiers coming down at them. Richard stumbled across the open field with the three Frenchmen. He reached the woods and hit the ground, hearing the rap of fire threatening them. The French took off in another direction, racing toward the path into the valley but a squad of Germans appeared and began firing at the three of them. The French hurled themselves onto the ground. Richard turned and took off into the woods, with no idea where he was going. He didn't know where Timmons was. He could hear the furious sounds of machine gun fire and artillery shells exploding down by the tracks where the Americans were being decimated.

Richard ran down a hill to the river below. He went through the underbrush, arriving at the tracks, where a string of boxcars was lining up at a siding.

He stopped. The small canal was much like the one beside

the tracks at home where as a kid he'd jumped freight for a ride out of town. He approached the door of an open boxcar, raised himself up, shimmied through the narrow opening, pulling himself inside. The space was filled with huge crates and boxes, the material rising to the roof – probably supplies for the front. A strong odor came from the deep recesses of the car, like rotting food.

He tried to slide the door shut but the thick wood frame wouldn't budge. Edging by the crates he settled down between two boxes that hid him.

The sound of gunfire sputtered in the distance; the GIs, he figured, were being rounded up by the encircling German infantrymen who had sucked the Patton invaders into a trap. Wounded and dejected GIs would be going back to Domburg as prisoners.

But for the moment he was free. Exhausted by his efforts, and musing about his prospects he drifted off to sleep.

Later in the early evening hours the freight jolted him awake, slamming his head against the sharp edge of a crate. The boxcars moved forward, stopped, jerked ahead, throwing him off-balance; then stopped. Again the sharp acrid odor hit him – stronger than rotting food. He figured there were dead rats in the straw.

Voices came from the tracks, the speakers coming closer until they were talking outside his car. Afraid they might start unloading material he crawled between two crates at the rear. The door was pushed open and a light sprayed the interior of the car, making odd shadows on the walls. Germans began questioning each other. Then they moved off, their light receding toward the front cars until it died down. The door was left open.

A violent jerk shook him and the line of freights slid along. A plane swooped down over the tracks, dropping several bombs that exploded on the sides of the boxcar. The American pilots, he figured, would assume the train carried supplies.

The cars stopped. Voices roused him again, coming from the

tracks outside. There was an argument between two Germans. The speakers approached; the ponderous door was slammed shut with a resounding crash and the bolt swung fast with a clang to lock it, so Richard was in the dark. A light flickered on and off outside, then disappeared. The voices faded away.

The freight moved on again and soon was whizzing along. Richard figured the train was heading east – loaded with civilians and soldiers fleeing from the advancing American forces.

Despite the rocking he decided to look out the window. Mounting one of the large crates and putting his foot on the side timbers of the car, he climbed high enough to reach the window. Balancing himself as the freight sped along, he stared out into the night as a flare lit up the surrounding area.

As the train shook the crates around him, he heard an odd sound in the car like bodies hitting the wood. In an extended flash tossed from the window, two shapes stood out against the distant wall – two civilians in heavy coats and wool hats. Were the Germans hiding from the authorities, seeking asylum to the east?

Planes were coming over and bombs began landing near the cars. He crouched on the top of the crate, sweating out the raid. Smoke came from the city and swirled over the car like a black river. More bombs fell and though he wanted to watch the fiery display at the window he wanted to hide from the figures at the back. Slowly he let himself down into the labyrinth of crates. Feeling a sharp jab in his chest, he twisted from side to side to get comfortable in the straw.

The two bodies were pushed about by the rocking of the train. Were they sick and dying or waiting to make a move against him? He felt around in the straw and managed to find a slat from one of the crates. He wondered if he should strike first.

The boxcars slowed down and stopped. Was this the end of his trip? A red fire from an exploding bomb lit up the window.

In the dying light he saw the faces of the two figures and

could distinguish the woman's hair, her coat open, revealing a tattered grey blouse. They seemed to be changing their positions and Richard crept around the crate which separated him from the couple. A light from the window flashed on and, as the train picked up speed again, the male appeared to be moving toward him. Alarmed he raised his stick and brought it down hard on the man's head. There was no cry. In the flickering light the face stood out – yellow, bloated, the eyes deep bits. The man's body gave off an odor that made him gag.

Going back to his hiding place he lay back on the floor, exhausted, feeling the first flush of a fever. In a short time he was boiling in the cold car. He felt a throbbing in his chest.

The planes returned and the bombs rained down as if rattled by a crazy hand; the shocks rolled under the car, adding a rumbling to the click-click of the wheels. He wondered if this fire-bombing of an enemy city was a foretaste of the devastation to come.

He lost all sense of time. How long had he been in the boxcar? he wondered. Maybe he was being crated like an animal in the cattle car to the crossroads where the two bitter armies would finish their bloodbath.

The end was coming; he would either be free or wiped out.

The early morning light came through the window above him and the two citizens stood out clearly, their bodies askew, necks bent at impossible angles, their limbs sprawled awkwardly like marionettes. As the car jerked they fell into each other like lovers. There was a bruising bloodless cut across the man's forehead from Richard's blow.

This must be the last German couple, he thought, coming to the end of the line.

The train came slowly to a halt. He heard shouting and the crack of small arms fire and he climbed up to the window and saw German soldiers racing from the train toward the trees beyond the siding.

Then a huge Russian soldier stepped out of the woods, wrapped in a cocoon of a loose coverall, a helmet crushing a white fur cap that left only the eyes free. The giant, followed by a squad of men, brought a submachine gun down and waved it at the fleeing soldiers as if to say, "Take off. I'll give you a running start."

Two of them ran across the tracks into the trees and the big Russian walked casually after them like a hunter going after his prey.

Richard heard shots; then the Russian came back out of the woods and lumbered toward the freight. Standing outside the car the soldier raised the machine gun, fired three times into the air, shouting in a shrill voice for those in the car, "*Heraus!*"

Richard moved down to the door and banged on the wood with his fist. In a few minutes the door was pushed open and two Russian soldiers looked in, keeping their guns on him. "American," he shouted. "American." They smiled but waved him out the door with their guns. Getting down from the car, he saw German civilians pouring out of the freight cars ahead of him, in small groups and families, who had fled the American saturation bombings only to be caught in the embrace of the Russian soldiers.

POWs began running out from the train onto the tracks, gathering around their liberator, cheering the odd colossus who, with a wave of her gun, had made all the Germans run for cover.

The Russian shouted again, in a high womanish voice, "All Americans are free thanks to the heroic Russian army."

Richard heard a familiar cry, "Yahooo!" and recognized Timmons who'd been recaptured and sent east with the other POWs – in the same freight Richard was in – the Germans wanting to prevent their rescue by the US Army.

A plane came over and swooped down, but the pilot didn't fire at them. The plane rose and banked, as he came in again to have another look at them. They stayed in place to signal they were Allied troops and the plane went over, almost in slow motion.

The pilot turned and came down slowly toward them. Their Russian liberator looked up at the aircraft; the fur cap tilted back and two long braids stood out. Timmons saw the suggestion of breasts above the soldier's tight belt, beneath the shoulder straps that held grenades and ammunition. The planes came at them and fired a burst, making them all hit the ground. The Russian stood firm and fired a round from the machine gun at the plane as it sailed by like a gull.

On the next sweep the plane came right over their heads. "It's a P-51," Timmons said. "They want to kill us." The plane passed on without firing.

"They can't tell who we are," Richard said.

The plane descended again and let out a burst of machine gun fire and a bomb squeezed out of the underside and floated down to the railroad yard. The POWs ran madly to the woods across the tracks. The pilot, as if sensing their panic, circled and came down again and sprayed them with a burst. Richard and Timmons raced as if they were in a hundred yard dash, and made it to the shelter of the trees.

After the plane disappeared, the Russian soldier led the POWs through town. The German civilians, soldiers, refugees – with the POWs – who had fled to the east to escape the encircling American troops, had been intercepted by this advance unit of the Russian army.

And now the Russian officer took off her helmet and fur cap, letting her hair fall about her neck, nodding to the Americans as if to show them a woman could fight in the front lines.

Richard was amazed how totally leveled the eastern town was. The Americans, he heard, had been bombing the town, and what buildings were left, the Russian artillery obliterated. Even without his glasses he made out the wide cracks in the streets, houses without walls, their rooms opened to the elements, with chairs and tables still in place. He'd write a poem about this ruined town.

Coming to the main street Timmons said, "You know, Richard, they say the women here in this town want GIs to come stay with them, protect them from the Russian soldiers who are raping the German girls."

"Would you protect them?"

"Yes. And they might be so grateful they'd let us spend the night with them."

"Timmons, that's revolting."

"What – protecting a lovely German girl from rape?"

"No, balling her yourself."

"Richard, you're such a Christer."

The Russian rounded up the POWS and took them to a railway station, motioning them to enter the waiting room. There the POWs found places on the floor and Richard lay down, feeling the steady pain in his chest. Yet he was still exhilarated at the thought he was free.

Before sleeping he wrote down a few lines of a poem:

The Ruins of a German Town

The grass is pushing up
through the cracks in the street
like flowers on a tomb.
Houses without walls
are stripped like naked women.
Chairs and tables, still in place,
resemble a house of dolls.

A cap drifts in a watery ditch
like an old love bobbing
in the mind's wake.
The moon banks
like a lost plane
giving a dangerous light
for the last soldier on guard.

Survivors who know
how the city looked
sweep up the ashes,
paint over the reddened walls,
carve out a road for the trucks
to haul off the dead
lying in awkward poses.

Then after all that blood
a rose outside our room
waves many flags
of white pink buds.
The perfumed lily
puts down its blooms
like markers on a grave.

A weary German crawls
out of the underground
his hair powdered with ash
like Goethe's ghost
and writes down that the war
turned all of them to stones
as hard as bullet shells.

Until at last, beyond
all the dumb dog days,
we can now lay down
a ring of tears
like a wreath
on all the stones
that we'd become.

The next day Richard and Timmons roused themselves, eager to find out when they would be returned to the American zone. Richard was anxious to get a doctor to check his wound.

Later one of the Russians who spoke English invited the ex-POWs to a ceremony on the hill, saying it was their privilege to observe the fate of the captured German officers.

They arrived at a graveyard where about twenty bodies were lying on the hillside, awaiting burial – mostly Russians, but a few GIs and a couple of civilians. The officers were quiet, looking out over the valley as if they were Hitler's victorious commanders. Their long pants were stained, their boots worn out. One wore a ski cap with a dirty green insignia; another wore high Russian boots he'd failed to get rid of before he was taken. A stern-faced Colonel had an Iron Cross dangling from his neck and a crushed battle ribbon on his breast. Their faces were unshaven, dirty.

On the hill they stood quietly in front of a shed, waiting for the first time in their lives to take orders from a woman, who asked a subordinate to strip the officers of any bars and braid and rip off the Iron Cross from the neck of the officer. She ordered them to take off their uniforms and, without complaining, the Germans removed their outfits, ending up in their odd woolen long underwear. Without any marks of rank, medals or guns, they looked like a bunch of tired old janitors. They were ordered up against a shed, where Richard figured they must've supervised the work of burying Russian prisoners, who, abandoned by their government, had died like flies.

Katrina, as the men called the Russian officer, stood in front of five Germans – staring at the face of the stern-faced Colonel, and suddenly Timmons recognized the paunch and short stumpy arms of Commandant Axel from Domburg.

She looked at the Russian corpses piled up beside the shed, hidden by their frozen overalls that made an instant shroud for them. Looking at the enemy officers she pointed to the graveyard: first to the Allied graves with only ten or eleven crosses; then to the Russian graves with hundreds of scattered indentations in the earth. Waving her arms back and forth from the Allied plots to the Russian, shaking her head in fury at the Commandant, she screamed, *why* – *"Warum? Warum?"*

Receiving no reply she spoke to a subordinate, who lined up the officers, blindfolded her with a handkerchief, placing her about five feet from the Germans. She took a gun from her belt, cocked it and pointed it in the direction of the condemned men.

"Ein, zwei, drei," the noncom counted off, mocking the defeated soldiers in their language. The officer fired, missing the target. The subordinate reported this to her and moving her within a foot of the Germans raised her arm so that it pointed at the nearest officer's chest. Again he counted, *"Ein, zwei, drei,"* and again she shot and a German fell.

One by one, missing once or twice, assisted by her Corporal, who raised or lowered her arm, and smiling like a child playing a game, she hit each of her targets. Two weren't hit in a vital spot and the Corporal finished them off with his rifle butt. The Germans didn't cry out or try to avoid the shots.

Then she came to the Commandant who, Timmons figured, couldn't be blamed for these dead prisoners since he had probably just arrived with the civilians from Domburg, perhaps relieved of his duties because of the breakout from the *stalag*. The Corporal told the officer that the Commandant stood in front of her. With her blindfold still on she waved toward the Russian mounds and screamed again, *"Warum, warum?"* With the Corporal guiding her hand she fired until the Commandant fell like a sack.

The GIs were amazed. When the avenging Katrina had finished her target practice she ripped off her blindfold, turned and scowled at the Americans as if resentful that they were alive while so many of her countrymen were buried there. Timmons whispered to a GI that he hoped the woman hadn't gone berserk.

She waved for the GIs to take the road back to the tracks and once there the Russians ordered them inside the German officers' quarters, a small house next to the railway station. Two GIs wandered off from the house and down the tracks. A Russian fired a burst from his machine gun over their heads until they stopped and ran back with the others to enter the house. They were all packed into a side room, well furnished with desks, maps and coffee tables. Richard and Timmons took places on the carpeted floor.

A GI came in and said, "I talked to that Russian who speaks English. He said a battle is raging for the town. He'll try to get food for us but they don't have much for themselves. He said we'll be locked up in this house for at least three weeks. Make no attempt to leave day or night, he told me, or they'll shoot us."

"The Ruskies are our enemy now," the GI said.

Richard was amazed. He'd heard other GIs say the same thing. Where did they get the idea? Would the next war be with the Russians? Did they have to pick a new enemy as soon as the old one passed on, to continue the cycle of death? But anyway, this war was over for them. There would be time now for celebration and a royal return to the States before the next conflagration.

On the Way Home

14

The train came to a halt in the station and Richard, unsure of his moves without his glasses, stepped down cautiously onto the platform. He'd lost touch with the other POWs when the Russians turned him over to a medical officer for treatment, who took Timmons and the remaining prisoners to the train for Paris.

Stumbling along, Richard moved toward the gates, ready for a good time but feeling like he was back in the bowels of the Penn Station when they'd walked through similar levels of hell to get to their troop train. His foot felt better. The medic who had driven him in an ambulance from the Russian zone to the train for Paris had given him new boots, and had cut out the toe of the left one to relieve the pressure on his bandaged foot. He also put a Band-Aid on Richard's shoulder scar, telling him it was completely healed. He cleaned and bandaged his chest wound, saying he ought to go to the Red Cross Center in Paris where they would give him an X-ray of his chest.

People were pushing each other on the platform and he was sucked into the undertow of bodies heading for the gates, holding on to the shiny manna of white bread he'd gotten in the ambulance. Soldiers and civilians in the sultry May heat were anxious to get out of the station. A slight woman in an army coat was shoved along on an equal basis with the men. The closer he got to Paris the filthier he felt in his dirty uniform, like a bum coughed up by the peace. He was swept along a grimy hall and down a stairway to a lower level; he stopped when he saw he was going the wrong way and doubled back against the tide. He found himself in a tunnel that curved under the station like the approach to a mine. The foul smell of coal gas made him cough. At the end of the tunnel he came to another dark level and eased into a stream of arriving soldiers of all nationalities, decrepit figures in torn, greasy-brown overcoats, shuffling along like orderly lost souls.

He arrived at a main gate and on the other side of a barrier ten or more civilians approached the returnees. An old man bolted past the ticket collector, hurdled a chain and ran up and down in front of the soldiers. Throwing his arms around one of the men, hugging and kissing him he shouted, "Garn, Garn." Then he held the soldier at arm's length, saw he'd made a mistake and drew back ashamed. A small Frenchwoman at the gate in a *babushka*, faded red coat and flowered hat stared at the faces of the incoming soldiers as if they were in a police lineup. She stopped in front of Richard and despite the fact that his uniform, even covered with grease, was American, shouted at him, "Max, cher Max?" He shook his head and she ran off. A ragged scarecrow emerged from the smoke – erect, sallow, bald with a straw-mottled beard and clothes that were ancient shreds. The small woman with the *babushka* ran to him, crying, "Max," and the old man confronted him too, calling, "Garn, Garn." Richard wondered who they saw in the scarecrow – son, husband, lover. He felt he'd witnessed the scene before – perhaps in a dream.

He emerged with a stream of returnees up a stairway, holding on to the rail to steady himself. Abandoning the herd he went through a door and was drawn into an enormous bright space. He drifted along with the crush of shoving bodies, passed through the door of the huge waiting room and came out into the blinding light of a Paris street – which made him shield his eyes. But there was a warm morning breeze, and he realized spring was coming.

A Red Cross truck was parked in the street and he figured the attendant might give him directions. A hand put cups on a board counter and a woman appeared, setting up doughnuts and a pot of coffee. He remembered getting off a train in Pittsburgh after months of confinement to the camp in Basic. A young woman in a white Red Cross uniform had given him a bag with a plain cake doughnut and a small paper cup of black coffee. "They think if they give you enough doughnuts," Timmons had said, "they'll take care of your sex life." On the train he had tossed his doughnut up onto the baggage rack like he was shooting a basket and the others laughed. Richard bawled him out. He was moved by these unforeseen gifts. From Pittsburgh to Indianapolis, whenever the train stopped, he looked for the Red Cross lady.

He got into a line forming at the side of the truck. The young woman in a crisp white uniform who looked out over the heads of the GIs was plain-looking, with a narrow, skeletal face. She made jerky robot-like moves as she set out cups, arranged the doughnuts and poured out coffee from the pot into a few of the paper cups.

He stared at her as she poured the coffee, motioning to the first GIs to take their portions. "Coffee here, doughnuts there," she said, intoning like a traffic cop. Her uniform was clean, freshly starched, but a button on her blouse had come loose. After Richard got his coffee and doughnut he hung around for a chance to talk to her. Waiting till the last GI had walked off, he moved up to the truck, hesitant. He wanted to hear her voice again.

"Are you American?" he asked.

"Yes. I'm a volunteer."

"You're the first American girl I've seen in a long time. What's your name?"

"Emily," she said. "Did you get your doughnut and coffee?"

He held up his uneaten doughnut and nodded toward his cup. "My name's Richard."

"Our group leader says if we take too much time with one person, then we won't have time for the others."

He didn't hear what she said – it was like a recording – but her voice captivated him like a popular song.

"Where's the Red Cross Center, Emily?

"Why didn't you say that's what you wanted?" She wrote down the address on a paper, gave him exact directions but told him the headquarters wouldn't be open yet.

He wanted to relax her. "I knew a girl whose job in the Red Cross was to measure the holes in the doughnuts – to make sure they were all the same size."

157

"Why are you telling me this?"

Alarmed, she turned back to the counter and he felt sorry he'd upset her.

Heading toward the street she had designated he began to shuffle as the walk had irritated his sore foot. Yet the pain in his chest had subsided. He felt good; he was free of guards.

It was now a bright sunny day, and a band came down the street, which was a colorful blur for him without glasses. He heard the trumpets blaring and drums beating as he hobbled to the edge of the street where soldiers from all the allied forces were parading by, erect and rigid as if they were going to war instead of celebrating its end. He had been enthralled by the parades as a kid when soldiers who had been at the front marched by his house. Now he'd been there and he felt like joining the marchers. A Frenchman lifted a bottle of wine to his lips, then gave Richard the bottle to drink. After he had drunk, the man hugged him and began crying and laughing as if the war with all its problems was worth it, to give him such a kick now that it was over. Richard was excited to be in Paris at such a moment.

He tried to keep up with the marchers despite his sore foot. Since he figured nobody knew English he sang, "Roll me over in the clover" and a French teenager pointed at him and said to a friend, "GI, GI."

He followed his directions until the wide street, lined with lovely green trees coming into bloom, flowed into a circle with the Arc de Triomphe in the center, ten streets coming together to make a star. He was swept along with people shouting, crying – carrying him like a stone from side to side. Cars were coming by, bumper to bumper, with the VIPs, like the Tournament of Roses he'd seen in the newsreels, where decorated floats in the shape of boats would sail by with a crew of long-legged models in swim suits.

His vision was blurred and the crowd seemed to churn about him like clothes in a washer, and he was hurled against the bumper of an Army jeep. A General sat in the back seat – a very handsome, good looking officer, Richard thought, in his resplendent, immaculate olive jacket, with a chest full of "salad dressing," and five stars shining on his cap.

Some in the crowd shouted, "Ike, Ike," and Richard, squinting to make out the General's face, was thrilled to be looking at the Supreme Commander, his cheeks slightly powdered, like their Captain's, to resemble a movie star.

The General was silent, his resolute jaw rigid, as if in a dream. Perhaps, Richard thought, he was embarrassed by all the cheering.

As the crowd continued to push against the jeep, even the General couldn't ignore Richard, who was impeding his progress, and warned his driver – a well-decorated mustached Corporal, who waved frantically for Richard to step aside. But he couldn't budge and a woman, thrown off balance, grabbed him around the waist and in an embrace they fell against the jeep. Afraid he'd be sucked under the wheels, Richard pushed the woman back and jumped up on the fender, and the driver shouted, "Get out of the way, you dumb son of a bitch."

Richard, facing the crowd, his feet dangling, pretended he couldn't hear and smiled at the citizens clambering about his feet. He imagined they were screaming because he had liberated them.

They came into the Place de la Concorde where the sun was heating up the hard surface of the square. Richard, sweating from the heat, figured he'd make his move and leapt off the car and was caught in another swirling wave of people.

He walked along the spacious streets, feeling suddenly giddy. He was free in Paris. And he would be going home. And what would they think of the collapse of his outfit? Would they be ashamed of his defeat? He had trouble visualizing faces, even his mother's and father's. He tried to conjure up Gloria's lovely face from the photo he'd destroyed in camp. He could conjure up her long legs, her breasts in the loose swim suit. But he couldn't make out her face.

He stopped at an outdoor restaurant around noon, and with the francs the medic had given him, he ordered a sandwich and a glass of wine.

Enjoying his meal and sipping his wine he got a pencil from the waiter and wrote on the side of the menu a poem to recall memories of home.

Recalling my Hometown

I see again the yard
where I ran naked screaming
in the spray of the sprinkler –

the school I struggled in,
learning how to read
magical words –

the corner store where a dis-
penser for a penny
slid a sourball down the chute –

the barbershop where Ted,
because I never learned to tip,
scalped me each month –

the house of Teacher Piney,

full bosomed, who for my prize
caressed my neck –

Cal's ice cream parlor,
an oasis between the boring school
and home, where we met

the giggling girls and over drinks
studied their budding breasts
and mocking looks –

the grassy park where Ginny and I,
unbuttoned, lay
the whole long summer day

the Moravian tower
from which our trombones
pealed their sad chorales –

the corner college bar
where we sang corny tunes
before we left for the Army,

and then so suddenly,
aware the war was on,
I left town for a time.

And now I see again the street,
the yard, the school,
the market, the barbershop,

Miss Piney's house,
the ice cream parlor, school,
the tracks, the living park,

the tower and college bar
where we sang of loss
before and after our youth.

The graves are there
where Barber Ted
and dear Miss Piney,

Fat Cal, the giggling girls
and Ginny – O my God –
bring tears to my dreams.

But, City, if you can,
take care of my youth,–
it's yours,

we're just old lovers
gone our ways –

*good night, remember
me.*

Then he wrote home:

Dear Family,

*I don't know whether this letter will reach you
before I do. I'm on my way home. I guess I won't be
able to tell you everything that happened to me.
Timmons thinks I'd better keep the unpleasant events to
myself. But I'm not ashamed of what I did at the front.*

*I just wrote a poem, remembering my life at
home, which I enclose.*

I'll call you the minute I arrive in the States.

*Mother, I have to make this letter short, so they
can send it out right away. But I embrace you.*

Love,
Richard

Next he wrote Gloria:

Dear Gloria,

*I'm coming home – thank God. And I'm dying to
see you again. I hope you got my last letter and thought
about what I said to you then.*

*I was caught up in a parade celebrating the
liberation of Paris and shoved by the crowd, I ended up
on the fender of a jeep. In the backseat was General
Eisenhower. And what a handsome man he is, so
young-looking. I can't really believe this happened to
me.*

*We did the right thing in coming over here. We
actually saw one of the young German girls who was
going to be burnt on orders of this maniac who runs the
country.*

I was able to survive all the unpleasantness

163

because I had the memory of your beautiful face.
   I won't say any more. I want this letter to go out
as quickly as possible. I'll see you soon.
   Love,
   Richard

After leaving the train in the early morning, Timmons made a quick stop at the Red Cross Center, to get some money and several free packs of cigarettes. Then he headed to the Champs-Elysées where a GI he met said there was "lots of action."

Once on the wide sunny ceremonial street he felt the excitement of being free in the popular city.

A tall woman walked up to him – in a plain white-and-black checkered dress, with a pale face and dark haunting eyes, her head close-cropped like the woman in the political camp.

"Hello," she said. "I saw you back there. I thought you'd be crushed by the crowd."

"I'm free!" he shouted.

"You want to have a good time?"

"Yes, yes."

"Then come with me. I speak English." She took his hand and led him across the square. "You'll be mobbed by the crowds. Everybody's going crazy since the liberation. They want to drink and forget everything that's happened."

They came to a tall, ornamental pyramid in the center of a square and entered a park, guarded by a large bronze statue of a horse with wings. She put her arm about his waist as they walked by an eight-sided pool with a limitless garden and the sign *Elysium* on a post.

He figured she must be a prostitute but he didn't care. He let her lead him along.

"You like me?" she said, raising her hand to her shaved head. He nodded. "My name is Annette – you want to go to my

164

room, have a good time?"

"*Oui*," he said. He wondered how much it would cost. He had one-thousand dollars worth of francs he'd gotten at the Red Cross Center for backpay.

As if reading his mind she said, "I do it for nothing. Just give me some American cigarettes." He took out the two packs the Red Cross had given him and handed them to her.

She pointed to a hotel. "See there, the Hotel du Monde. Go and sign up for room thirty. Tell the elevator boy Karl that Annette's coming. Give him enough francs for a bottle of Calvados. I'll see you there." Leaning up, she kissed him on the cheek and he smelled a rich lilac odor.

At the hotel he signed the registry and in the elevator gave the boy Karl the message and the francs for the Calvados.

Once in the high-ceilinged room he hurled himself on to a four-poster bed with clean sheets and looked out the window letting in the light of Paris. He bounced up and down on the bed, shouting, "I'm free, free" until he was out of breath and fell back on the pillow, rolling off the bed to the floor, where he lay flat, swatting the balls of white fluff that had come off the cheap thick carpet and staring at the ceiling with its nymphs blowing trumpets, swaying above him as if they might swoop down on him.

The elevator boy brought in a tray with the Calvados and Timmons tipped him. After the waiter left he filled a glass full of the alcohol and drank it in one gulp. He went to the john where he ran the water into an antique tub that had a pump handle with snakes crawling over it. When the tub was full he stripped and got in; and the hot water sent a shock through his swollen foot and made his chest tingle. Looking at his body in the clear water he realized how thin he was. He remembered the cold, clammy shower he'd taken in Domburg with the other prisoners. He lathered himself luxuriously with the soap and sank into the suds.

He would be going home. In the contentment of the warm water he played his favorite home movies in his head, long blurred by prison life: drinking a draught of beer with friends; eating a barbequed rare steak; riding in an open car by the sea with a young redhead; swimming at night in the buff with the same redhead; shouting at a football game, the autumn air heavy with smoke from the burning leaves; skiing down the slopes at Stow with his friends, the wind buffeting their faces; dancing all night to a jazz trio with a tall, languorous woman who knew how to let herself go.

Half awake he looked up and saw Annette framed in the doorway, with only a black skirt on, a hand over her breasts as if embarrassed. She came and knelt by the tub, picked up the sweet smelling jasmine soap and paddled it on his chest, getting foam, and slid her smooth hands along his shoulders and down the side of his body. She was younger than he had thought at first. Her sad eyes reminded him again of the woman behind the barbed wire.

Helping him out of the tub she draped a large purple towel about his waist and began drying him. In the bedroom she undressed and got under the sheets, her head poking out like it was on a guillotine block. He sat on the edge of the bed with just a towel over him; then picked up his bottle of Calvados. He could smell the sweet jasmine on his body.

She pushed the sheets back and opened her arms to him. But he saw the breasts of the woman in the political camp. He poured her a glass from the bottle.

"Annette," he said, raising his bottle in a toast. "Bonne santé." She lifted her glass, and they drank.

"What are you waiting for?" she asked.

On an impulse he got his wallet and sitting on the bed, gave her a packet of francs. "For you," he said.

She handed the money back to him. "No, I do it for nothing. Just the cigarettes."

"Why?"

"You came up to me in the street and smiled. I looked like hell. You didn't make fun of me like most GIs." She pulled his towel away and laughed, "Come on. Why are you sitting there

166

like a satyr? You want something special? I had a German who wanted me to crawl around on my belly. But I don't hate him. The French set fire to my hair – they were so pure. Come on, – you don't think I'm ugly, do you? I'll take care of you."

He got into the bed and caressed her – which made her laugh. He kissed her and suddenly she pulled him on top of her and clamped him in a vise-like grip with her legs. He couldn't wait and entered her and came immediately. But she held on to him in a fierce embrace and his lungs pumped so ferociously she released him, saying, "Are you okay?"

He got the bottle of Calvados and relaxing drank till his throat was scorched. His head spun and he put the bottle down, holding on to her, looking up at the claws of a tiger on the backboard of the bed. She had sent a shiver of well-being through him with her powerful grip. Prison life hadn't dried him up.

God, he thought, maybe there was a reason for all the shit he'd been through, if he could feel this way about the new life ahead of him.

He wanted to tell the world how happy he was. He got up and though Annette tried to bring him back to the bed he went out into the hall and, holding the bottle up like a pistol shouted, "Everybody out!" In the sultry hall he didn't care that he was naked. He knocked on the first door, yelling, "Everybody out. Paris is liberated." He banged on the second door, yelled, "*Aux armes, O Citoyens*," and a man came to the door and looked out with disgust. A woman came from another room and seeing him, roared with laughter. She stepped into the hall with only her panties and a bra on and did a mad dance to encourage him and followed his naked figure, bumping and grinding. She bowed to him and took off her bra like a stripper and he bowed to her and offered her his arm for a dance. She took it and they did a two step until a man came out of her room and chased them, pulling her back against her will, pushing her laughing and screaming into their room.

Returning to his room he found three people standing outside his door. A heavy-set man, wearing what looked like a toupee, was pointing at him, leading the angry chorus. Timmons raised his bottle to toast him, *"Bonne santé."*

"Vous êtes fou," the man said, shaking his head as if Timmons was wild, and rushed to seize him. He ducked into his room and locked the door. Annette, afraid of trouble, was dressing quickly.

"Monsieur, open up," the man shouted from the hall and Timmons pushed a bureau against the door, knocking over his bottle and spilling Calvados on the rug. A key turned in the door and somebody pushed it in but couldn't budge the dresser. He looked in the mirror at his naked figure, so thin and wasted. Frightened, he went to the door and shouted, "Go away, or I'll shoot. *Partez ou je tire."*

It was quiet in the hall and he heard the word *"gendarme."* Afraid they might get the police he dressed in a hurry. Waiting for the crowd to leave he smiled at Annette who was waiting to get out.

"You're crazy," she said, "but you're a good fellow. Come again. Ask my friend in the elevator to call me. We'll go to the beach sometime."

When all was quiet outside he opened the door and she rushed out, disappearing in the direction of the elevator. He left too, going the other way to the stairs that led to the floor below his. A repair man in overalls saw him and scowling shouted, *"Cochon."* Timmons ran down a long hall, found a window open, and let himself out. He landed on the cement below, got up and ran down an alley, where he saw a policeman at the corner, and slowed to a walk. He must be careful. The memory of the French chasing him through the halls had sobered him.

The officer disappeared into the crowd and Timmons left the alley for the main street. The afternoon sun was blazing, and feeling free he let out his cheer, "Yahoooooooooooooooooo!"

15

At the Red Cross Center that afternoon Richard signed the registry, adding his name to the "Agony Grapevine" of returning POWs. He made an appointment for a medical exam and signed up for a ship home. Everything was speeding up.

Before his physical he got a bed in the dorm, a shower, fresh khakis, a VD kit, and a thousand dollars worth of francs. After a cursory eye check by an army optometrist he got a pair of glasses as close to his old prescription as could be arranged. He finally could see clearly people's faces.

When his turn came he went to the medical room and a nurse met him at the doctor's office – a bouncy, short, dark-haired woman with an oval face.

"Richard," she said, "come on in. The doctor's ready. I'm Kathie. I've been assigned to the shuttle ship that's taking you home so you'd better get used to me."

"I'm glad to meet you. I just got my glasses. I can see you."

"That's wonderful."

The doctor, a grey-haired, self-effacing man, checked him out and Richard told him about the gnawing sensation in his chest where the shrapnel had hit him. The doctor put a fresh bandage on his chest and sent him for X-rays.

He waited in the anteroom for a few hours until the nurse Katie came by. "What's the verdict?" he asked.

"That's the question," she said. "Like 'to be or not to be?' The doctor wanted me to talk to you. Call me Miss Ambiguity 1945. Well, your left foot's gotten larger than your right. You'll need special shoes. Also, there's a mystery spot on your lung. You said you got hit by shrapnel. They're going over your X-ray photos."

"Richard, can I ask you a few questions? A friend of mine at the *New York Post* asked me to help him write an article on veterans like yourself – reporting what they went through, how the war affected them and how they'll adjust to civilian life. He's also writing a novel and will use the highlights from our article for his story – so the whole world will hear about your exploits. Will you help me with the article?"

"Okay."

"We'll have several interviews. But right now, would you tell me – what was the worst thing that happened to you in the war?"

"Well, if you ask me it was the concentration camp we passed. We saw a short young girl in a prison outfit, half naked, her head shaved. The rumor was that she was one of the gypsies they were going to burn. I wrote a poem about it."

"Let me hear it."

"It's my imaginary version of what happened."

He took out his paper and read:

A Song for the Gypsy

In the crowded concert hall
a woman is singing
a song of Hafiz –
"Now when the violin
forgives the past,
it will start singing."

Then in my mind I hear
the cracked violin wailing
a Moorish song
for the Gypsy girl
about to be burnt –
a short, black-skinned girl,
naked with a blood-red scarf
which binds her long black hair,
a strand of necklaces
about her breasts,
and tiny red shoes

170

on which she's swaying
to the cry of the violin,
which holds off for a while
her burning.

Meanwhile the one-armed guard
who's piling up straw
tries to turn away
from his duty
of "doing this one"
outside the oven.

And from the camp's door
I see her shoes catch fire;
the flame flares up
and sweeps across her hair;
a woman screams;
the children cry out
and dogs bark madly.

I think if now,
as Hafiz wrote,
the violin forgives the past,
maybe it can sing
for the Gypsy girl
so even at this late hour
her star might rise
in the enchanted night sky.

"That's a lovely poem. Now I have a few more questions, and then I have to interview some other ex-POWs.

After talking with the nurse, Richard went to the Rec. room where there was to be a variety show, and suddenly ran into Timmons. "Hello, buddy," he shouted. "I got glasses and I can see you now."

"I must look like hell," his friend said.

"No, you look great – with a shave and new clothes. What happened to you?"

"Well, I had a woman in Paris. Her name was Annette, with dark eyes, almost bald. I think she fraternized with the Germans and the French shaved her head. We drank Calvados and she gave me a hot bath. Then she did the deed for nothing, just a few cigarettes because she said I was nice to her. Later I was so drunk I walked naked up and down the hall. They called the police and I just got out of the hotel in time."

"Sounds like fun," Richard said. "I met a Red Cross girl who thought I was trying to make out with her. I got in a victory parade on the Champs Elysées and nearly got run over. I had to jump up on the fender of a jeep to keep from being crushed by the crowd. And guess who was sitting in the back seat – all quiet and subdued – General Eisenhower."

"So he was being hailed as the liberator of Paris?"

"Yes. Isn't that something to write home about?"

"I guess so."

The afternoon show began, interrupting their talk and the hall filled up with GIs, including an assembly of amputees: one with an arm gone; another with a leg missing; a third with a leg and an arm off; another with two legs and an arm missing; and one with no limbs at all, pushed along in a wheelchair by a friend. The amputee next to Richard took off his legs and folded them under the seat to be more comfortable as half a man. He explained to Richard that when he put the legs on, the metal cut into his skin. "It takes time," he said, "before you get a new one that fits."

A dwarf came out on the small stage from behind a makeshift curtain – with a long nose and red cheeks, in a huge yellow-and-blue checkered sports coat that came down to his knees.

"Welcome home, GIs," he shouted with an odd fey twang. "Take a real hug and kiss from all of us at the USO troop. I hope you get that big boat home as soon as possible. I see you hugging your loved ones as you get back to the America you dreamt about in the prison camps – the America of free enterprise. We have a good show for you, sponsored by the Lucky Strike company. And this show is a special for you guys who gave a hundred percent and put Hitler back in his cage."

The troops began shouting, "Sheila, Sheila, we want Sheila," the name of the woman on the posters. The entertainer came out on the stage, a pleasant woman with powder on her cheeks, her hair done up in pigtails like a child. It took guts, Richard thought, to walk out into a den of horny GIs.

"I'm going to sing an aria," she said. "It's called *Un Bel Di* which means 'one fine day he will return.' And that's what your loved ones are singing right now." The men groaned at the thought of an opera song but Timmons applauded. He didn't care what she sang. He was free, out of the cold woods, and on his way home. He thought of Annette at the hotel, smelled again the odd jasmine soap and felt again her vise-like grip that had brought him back to life.

The GIs were quiet during the aria but when the singer was through, a GI yelled, "Sing 'Far Away.'" An English sailor shouted, "Give her a chance, lads." The GI replied, "Blow it out, old chap."

"I don't know that song, honey," the singer said.

"Then take it off," a GI said, and to be a sport she slowly rolled off her gloves, to mock applause.

Halfway into the next aria the soldiers began pounding on the tables and screaming, "Take it off, take it off."

"Let her sing," Richard shouted.

"Blow it out yours," a GI answered.

The singer stopped, unsure what to do. The table pounding went on, the soldiers began booing and she rushed offstage. The dwarf came back and unruffled by the confusion said in his squeaky voice, "LSMFT, LSMFT, LSMFT."

The sound was maddening and Richard, unnerved, got up and headed for the aisle to get out of the hall.

"LSMFT, LSMFT, LSMFT, LSMFT," the dwarf went on. "LSMFT, LSMFT, LSMFT."

"Stop it!" Timmons shouted from the aisle and two men in the front row rushed towards the platform. The small man, seeing them come, as if he expected the attack, reached into his pocket and took out packages of cigarettes and called out, "Lucky Strike means fine tobacco. LSMFT, LSMFT, LSMFT." The dwarf tossed packs into the air and the first men coming onstage to throttle him bent down to pick up as many packs as they could. To stop the deluge the salesman took out more packs from a box and repeating his insane incantation tossed them high into the air. The amputee who had his legs under the seat heaved himself into the aisle and crawled toward the flying packages. Others dove or swam across bodies to get the prizes, forgetting their mechanical limbs.

Richard struggled to the exit. Outside the Rec. room he felt a sudden shooting pain in his chest and went quickly to his sleeping quarters. Lying back in the bed he massaged his wound to ease the pain. He took several deep breaths and held on to the side of the bed. He finally lost consciousness but the pain made him groan in his sleep.

He dreamt he had arrived home and his father was taking his duffel bag. His mother called down from upstairs and asked if the prodigal had returned. Then he was in the dining room that had been decorated with pictures of crosses in a field of poppies, honoring his father's war. They were eating and his father called to him from the other side of the table, "So many boys never came back. I'm sorry you were beaten by the

Germans and taken prisoner."

Later in the early evening, by the light from the door, he made out the dark-haired nurse Kathie, who was sitting on his bed, holding his hand. "What are you mumbling about, old fellow?" she asked.

"I had a dream."

"I don't know much about dreams. Mine are obvious, losing things, running from Big Nurse, getting in and out of bed with the wrong guy. What was bothering you?"

"The dwarf at the Rec. center."

"The hell with him. Remember – you're going home."

"That's right. I've had trouble visualizing people back home. But I'm beginning to remember what they looked like."

She bent over to cover him up and her breasts ran across his shoulder. "Maybe you need a rub, to relax you."

"Sure. I'm stiff."

She got him to roll over; then put an oil on his shoulders and began to give him a rubdown. "Tell me what you've been doing in Paris."

"I ended up in a parade and imagined they were cheering me."

"And they should've been. You guys went through a hell of a lot."

She finished the massage and sat on the edge of his bed. "I shouldn't be sitting on your bed," she said. "If Big Nurse caught me, she'd roar, 'Off with her head.' We'll talk later. Right now, I've got to go."

"Thanks for the rubdown. I felt I was falling to the bottom of a well – and you pulled me out."

"I'm glad. You're on my hit list. And we'll talk more about your article. But I got a thousand other guys to check on." She took his head between her hands. "You don't want a pig in a poke, do you?"

He'd never heard anyone talk like that and he burst out laughing.

16

Richard and Timmons found out their ship would leave the next morning and they had a final day to explore what was left of Le Havre.

Before they could get out of the barracks a Lieutenant read an order for all POWs to gather in the field for calisthenics and work details. The order had come from a General who had just arrived at the Center. It turned out that it was their Division Commander, Whistling Willy, whose reputation as "The Purple Heart General" had spread throughout France.

The men, called out to the field, bitched to the Lieutenant in charge, some refusing to do the exercises. Richard tried to lift his legs high when running in place but he lost his breath and had to sit down.

When the General left the area, the Lieutenant in charge handed out passes to everyone. "Get the hell out of here," he said, "until your ship sails."

Richard and Timmons bought some cheese and bread at the PX and headed for the gates. On their way out they ran into the General's limousine. As it passed, Timmons yelled out, "Oh hello there, General." The car stopped, backed up and the General rolled down his window and called to them, "Who made that noise?"

"What noise?" Timmons said.

"Why aren't you fellows at drill?" the General asked.

"We're on a work detail," Timmons said. "We're going to clean up the rubble outside the gates."

The officer, whose eyes were too small for his broad face, stared at Richard's boot that had been ripped apart. "What happened to that boot?" he asked.

"A medic cut it apart, so my foot would fit into it. I had frostbite."

"What was the medic's name?"

"Krankenhaus, or Eisenheimer."

"Try to remember, soldier. Nobody has a right to destroy

government property."

"Thank you for your interest, General. At the front my left foot began to throb. One medic said, don't touch it; stay off your feet. The foot got beet red and hurt like hell. Another person said, rub it with spit and keep moving. Well, my left foot got swollen and it's larger than my right. A medic cut the toe out of this boot to fit my enormous foot."

"General," Timmons said, "why did the army send us those soft hide boots? Ninety percent of our division got frostbite because of that decision."

"The men forgot to grease their boots."

"We didn't have any grease at the front, General. In fact we didn't have anything – tank support, food, water. Our division was wiped out."

"What outfit were you with?"

He took off his jacket and pointed to the growling lion on the shoulder patch of his shirt. "I was in your outfit, General."

"You men held the enemy back; you gave General Eisenhower time to counterattack. Thank God we were part of that great effort."

"No, General. You weren't there. That's not how it worked. You see, the Germans secretly built up an armada of *Volksgrenadiers* right across from us. Our Intelligence thought they had all gone south."

"You didn't see the whole picture."

The General, anxious to make his escape from the questioning, urged his chauffeur to drive on.

"Maybe you could help us, General," Richard said. "Our captain, name of Plankton, of I Company, the 506th, was taken somewhere by the German guards. There was talk in the camp the Captain was selling GI food parcels to the enemy. We heard he may have offended the guards."

"That sounds like a vicious rumor," the General said.

"Have you heard what happened to Captain Plankton?"

"It so happens we have. The Germans for some reasons let the Russians have him. We've sent a formal demand for his release."

"Why would they hold him?"

"When they liberate a camp they often send American POWs to Russia. They hope to exchange them for Russian deserters held by the Allies."

Timmons wanted to ask him how it felt to take an untrained division into combat and lose it in a couple of days. But he remembered how the General got his nickname, Whistling Willy, when the troops on a field march had passed a golf course and saw the General with an attractive woman and whistling as he walked along the fairway.

"General," Timmons said. "I heard you were quite a golfer back in the States."

Motioning his driver to go on, he replied, "Get to work, you two."

"Ass," Timmons said to the departing car.

They went out of the Embarkation Center gate and walked to the top of a hill overlooking Le Havre. They sat down and ate their food, looking down at the seaport town that had been bombed by Allies and enemy alike, long after there was anything but rubble to churn up. The famous town, that once had lovely parks and high apartments, was dust. In one building, with three sides missing, they could see tables turned upside down and blackened furniture still in place.

There were no women in the town, no children playing in the puddles that had multiplied below the broken drainpipes. Fresh sprouts of grass were just beginning to squeeze out of the huge blocks of cement tossed about by the saturation bombing.

Walking back down the hill they came up to a section miraculously untouched by the bombings, with a row of stores and a café, which looked like a fake set against the backdrop of deserted fields. In a jewelry store Richard saw a window display of a mannequin in a long white dress with a purple turban, gold bracelets dangling from her wrist, jeweled pins on the front of her dress. It was an enlisted man's tourist trap but he figured he ought to get a souvenir from France – maybe something for Gloria. He and Timmons went in, and a clerk popped up from behind a register like a puppet, with a red line around her lips in the shape of a heart. She was wearing many of the same bracelets that she was selling and had diamond pins on her long red dress.

After looking around, Richard pointed to a brooch in the shape of an animal that resembled an antelope, whose neck was embellished with a heart-shaped cluster of glittering stones.

"You want a gift for your girlfriend?" the woman asked. "That's a sitatunga. It sleeps under water. Isn't it *magnifique*? See how the stones sparkle like real diamonds and rubies. Your sweetheart will love it."

Richard gave her the francs, figuring he was being gypped, but he didn't care. The saleswoman wrapped the animal as a present and as they left, he heard her laughing.

They went into the café next door and Richard ordered a beer and Timmons ordered two shots of gin. A small raised platform made a stage and a show was going on for the few GIs at the tables. Two dancers, one tall, one short, were bumping frantically, without grace, singing in high voices, "Ding, ding-a-ling, ding; ding, ding-a-ling, ding; fire, fire, fire." The two jumped about, their breasts popping out of their tight low-cut firemen's jackets. Finishing their number they stopped, turned their backs on the audience, and removed their tops. Turning around they stood still like statues; then turned and put their tops back on. Facing the GIs they bowed and danced off as if they were activated by their clothes.

When they got back to their quarters in the late afternoon they found that mail was being handed out. Richard got two letters and Timmons one. Richard opened the first from his

179

family:

Dear Richard,

We haven't heard from you in a long time. What are we to make of your silence? We learned you were a prisoner but some POWs have been able to send letters to the U.S.

Yet I imagine a young man in a distant clime, who has taken on a powerful enemy. We are only sorry you never became an officer.

The New York Times is full of stories of your battle, – Winston Churchill called it the Battle of the Bulge, –"the most famous battle of the war."

They say your Division stopped Hitler's move into Belgium. You are considered a bona fide hero here at home.

Everyone's talking about General Eisenhower. It's amazing what he's accomplished by his brilliant European strategy, destroying in such a short time the last remnants of the German army. What a terrific man. He's so popular there's talk of considering him for President.

So much has happened. I don't want you to come back and find out from someone else. Mother passed on in February after a brief illness. I won't go into details except to say it was a cancer related to her reproductive organs. I miss her. All my life, as you know, I've tried to do what was best for her. Even in her last days she was a mystic. As the Irish conjuror Yeats said, "A woman embraces an idea like a child of stone." She said at the end I abandoned her. But I will always remember the young woman in a straw hat, holding my arm when I was Captain of my ship.

When you come back you'll find things have changed. Some of your friends have gotten married. Others have graduated from college and gone on to careers in medicine and law.

I've talked to Mayor Tidings about a reception in your honor at Soldier's Park. He'd speak and they'd have an honor guard, and a local band performance.

Meanwhile, wherever you are, we hope you're in good health, with renewed confidence in your accomplishments – as mother said, always looking on the bright side.

Just between us, I've heard various odd rumors about the bad treatment of prisoners in Germany. I suggest to you, Rich, that if anything unfortunate or disturbing happened to you, I'd prefer that you don't tell anybody about it.

Love,
Dad

The news hit him like a body blow. His family had become a dim blur of faces, out of an old photo album but he always remembered his mother as a young woman in her straw hat who played with him at the beach during a long summer day. He realized his father too had kept alive that picture of his young wife.

Yet as he thought again of the letter he wondered why his father was so insistent that he shouldn't talk about anything unfortunate or disturbing that had happened to him.

He opened the second letter, from Gloria:

Dear Richard,

This is a difficult letter to write.

I was moved by your letter. I know you must've gone through some tough times over there. And I respect what you've done.

I wish I could be your wife. You are a fine person and I'm just a simple farm hand. I don't understand your poetry about Venus rising from the sea. I think you'd be bored out of your skull if we were

181

together even for a couple of months.

But if we're honest, Richard, you and I were never really a couple. We never even kissed. I guess with your love of poetry you made a romantic thing out of our relationship.

I have to tell you something else. Rollo first proposed to me while skiing in Aspen, Colorado, and I was mean, I laughed. How could I get married, I thought, since I have so much to experience? But I figured one has to decide some things sooner rather than later. So we finally tied the knot. He's out of the air corps for a liver ailment. He always regretted he couldn't get overseas where the action was.

I hope you are in good shape. I have a girlfriend who likes poetry and is dying to meet you, if you haven't fallen for any Frauleins yet. Such things happen in wartime, I understand. This boring stupid war has gone on too long. It has upset a lot of good times.

By the way, tell Timmons that Jolly's anxious to see him. She broke up with her guy and would like Timmons to give her a buzz when he gets back.

I can't think of much else to say.

My best,

Gloria

Timmons, after reading his letter, said to Richard, "I got a note from Jennifer. She said she misses me."

"Gloria says Jolly wants you to call her when you get home."

"Really. Maybe I will if the old fire's still burning. What was your news?"

"My father was upset I haven't written more. My mother passed on."

"Sorry to hear that."

"He said you and I are heroes."

"What B.S.!"

"And another thing. Gloria's married."

"I predicted that. You're lucky to be rid of her."

"It's hard for any woman to wait a long time for somebody to come back from the war. And she's been tempted by this guy, Rollo. But I'll never forget her. I dreamt about her all the time. And I wrote a few good poems about her."

"The Gloria you dreamt about doesn't exist."

"I don't know. I'll look her up when we get back."

They took an evening walk, both quiet, contemplating their return home. On the way back to the Center they passed the American graveyard and a crescent-shaped mausoleum, a grim cement pillbox. They walked into the mausoleum and found a long dark corridor leading to a chapel. On a desk outside the chapel was a large book containing the names of all the GIs buried in the outside graves, with numbers that would identify each dead GI. On the porch of the chapel was a symbolic casket with a permanent jet flame rising between two black pillars. A special plaque listed the names of those buried there who had made the journey all the way from Stein.

Leaving the mausoleum they came to the graveyard and the bright-green manicured lawns, with rows and rows of crosses stretching far back into the countryside. The sun held the picture in a frame of hundreds of crosses, the names recorded on the marble – GIs like those Richard had known: The Sergeant, Groaner, Henderson, Watson, Rabbit, and Rule.

They noticed a wedding taking place in the courtyard next to the church cemetery.

He wrote a poem that night:

The Military Cemetery

Walking to his ship
he passed the GI graves –

183

the walls around the churchyard like a fort
as if in death
the GIs must defend
themselves against
a fresh attack.

Above the chapel wall
he saw the crosses
made of shrapnel shells
picked up on the battlefield,
with the names of friends
who'd made the trip
from the front –
Henderson, Watson
Rabbit and Rule,
who hadn't wanted
their names on a plaque.

A jet flame rose
from copper candlesticks,
like nuns guarding
the dead GIs.
Outside the church
he came to the pristine
cared-for lawns
with row on row
of sturdy marble crosses
bearing the names of those
recorded on the plaques.

A married pair walked
onto the lawn –

a mustached man
in sparkling tux,
his bride full-veiled,
as white as snow –
who shielded their eyes
from the rain of rice.

A member of the wedding
was urging them
to stand rock-still
for photographs,
the chapel there
confining them,
the gravestones rolling
like waves
in the undulating
field of grass.

The cheerful living ones
who framed this scene
could not forget that men
whose graves were stretched
far into the countryside
had been so newly trans-
ferred by the way
into that other, secret
campground of the dead.

17

The next morning the old British liner, recently brought out of mothballs, eased out of the channel, avoiding the masts of sunken ships that had settled into the watery bath like toys.

After an hour out at sea Richard saw black clouds coming and the ship rose and fell like a seahorse, creaking and bending to the lashing. To resist the rolling and the nausea from the lack of balance the men sat on the deck or stretched out on reclining chairs or went down to their bunks to work out their sickness in private.

Kathie came up to Richard's desk chair. "It's rush, rush," she said. "I've just got a second. That storm – it's got everybody tossing bricks. And we don't have enough medicine. Here, if you're bored you can borrow my book." She showed him a leather-bound notebook and opening it said, "Try this one. 'I can resist anything but temptation.'"

"Is that you talking or the book?"

"That's for you to find out. Here's another – 'Men are like grapes; you get all kinds in a bunch.'"

"I had a girl back home. She wanted to know if I was a good investment. What's the book say about that?"

"It says –'love is a bad investment, if you think it's a business.'"

"I got some news. My mother died."

"I'm sorry to hear that."

"And my girlfriend – well, she wasn't really my girlfriend I guess – she got married."

"Good riddance."

"I still see her in my imagination. She kept me going during everything that happened to me."

"That's good. I'll put that in our article."

She took out her much-soiled book and opening it to a marked page said, "Listen to this. 'It often happens that after a particularly terrible experience,' –like the one you had, – ' a soldier may actually feel that he's lost his soul.'"

"What is the soul in your opinion?"

"According to my book the soul is something that gives you hope. And it's my job to make sure you get yours back."

"I don't think I've lost mine."

"We'll have another session. I must run. See you later."

After she left he heard a familiar voice coming from the forward deck and following the sound discovered it was Brother Bob from the camp, giving a talk – immaculate as before, a plaid scarf wrapped tight around his neck to protect his voice from the sea wind. A small group of GIs sat at his feet.

"I remember many of you from the prison," he said. "Some of our friends were taken from us. Only Jesus knows why. The war was brutal but could we let the evil in Germany go unchecked? Now I ask you to accept Jesus as your savior. He brought us out of the captive land."

Richard noticed how respectful the GIs were to the preacher, compared to the razzing some gave him in the warehouse. Did the man really mean what he was saying?

The steady rocking of the ship soured Timmons' mood. Walking on the deck of the dilapidated English troopship he saw the ghosts of all useless wars. At the railing a GI approached him – a hard looking fellow with a pockmarked face and eyes that had the charcoal circles of veterans who had been in too many firefights.

He looked over at the soldier, who turned his black-rimmed eyes on him, as if expecting a dumb remark.

"Hello," Timmons said.

"What?" the man said, in a harsh, unreal voice.

"I said, hello."

"Why did you say that? I've never seen you before and you act like you know me. Do you think I come out on deck to have a dumbfuck wasted son of a bitch say hello to me? I see by your insignia you were with that chicken outfit that threw in the towel in the Ardennes. It's an insult to be on the same ship as you. I hit the beaches in Africa. I have a hundred pieces of shrapnel in me. Almost everyone in my outfit was killed. You shouldn't be in the same world with me. I've got to keep my head clear. No, don't reply, or I'll toss you overboard."

Timmons didn't want to fight. The guy was screwed up – he might even have a knife. So he moved away from the railing.

Kathie came up to him and asked for an interview, for her article. "I'm all yours," she said. "I'm all ears too. I want to hear everything. Tell me what happened to you."

"Is this part of the therapy?"

"Yes. But I have to tell you something. I just saw my first death on this ship. I shouldn't tell you. I was sitting by this GI, feeling his pulse and it stopped just as a clock stops ticking. I asked the doctor why he died – we didn't think there was anything life-threatening – and he said 'because he couldn't live any longer.' Now I don't want you to stop ticking. So you got to talk."

"I don't want to shoot off about myself."

"I understand. You had a tough time at the front, and in the POW camp. Can you tell me about it?"

"So you can write an exciting article for *The Post?*"

"Hey, give me a break. I need your story. The other POWs won't utter a peep."

"Well, what happened at the front was a waste of time. For all the good I did I might just as well've stayed home and played football."

"What was it like in prison camp? Was there any one thing that upset you?"

"I saw this short woman, practically naked, bald-headed – I really can't talk about it."

"Tell me about her."

"She was washing her clothes in the stream. Later we smelled this stench that tasted sweet on the tongue. I figured they were burning civilians killed in the raids. But a

Frenchman said the Germans were burning their own people like this gypsy girl."

"Your buddy, Richard, told me about that. Why would they burn her?"

"I don't know."

"How did it affect you?"

"It made me realize man is a ridiculous, mean son of a bitch."

"I understand. But wouldn't you like everyone to know what you did for your country? People should know your story."

"Everything I did at the front was abysmally stupid. Tell that to the readers of *The Post*."

Just after midnight one of the nurses came into the room and slipped into Timmons' cot, still in uniform. She had trouble keeping in place beside him with the violent heaving of the ship. Playfully she put her fingers on his lips. She helped him take off his khaki shorts and edging along his side kissed him and whispered, "Let me do all the work."

He held her close, kissing her but she initiated the moves. He wondered if Richard in the other cot could hear them thrashing about. A light flashed on from the hall and he saw her slide her skirt up to her waist. She was over him, guiding him in and she rolled back and forth. He pulled her to him and as he came he was fighting for his breath. As he rested she kept up her rowboat motion until she came, then lay beside him and hummed a love song in his ear.

She leaned over and kissed him as if she would devour him. "Sorry I couldn't do it in the buff, especially in this heat. But, as they say, we have to be in uniform at all times."

"When do I see you again?"

"When I want to."

After she left, Timmons turned to Richard, "Are you awake?"

"What do you think – with all that screwing?"

"I didn't plan on it. I lucked out. Imagine – I just met her this afternoon. But she knew what I needed."

"Don't give me that. I had to listen to you in the camps – a woman gives you a sense of well-being. Is that all you got out of prison life? Get laid; clean out the pipes. You got sex on the brain, like a bee buzzing in there. I wish I could be as simple as you."

"Well, I can screw that nurse and forget how stupid everything was. And I'm not ashamed of enjoying a woman."

Richard had trouble sleeping that night. After rolling and tossing, trying not to get sick as the ship bucked and dove, he felt a round object like an onion stuck in his throat, cutting off his breath. He curled a finger behind his tongue to pull out the obstructing object but couldn't locate it. Nauseated by the onion smell he gagged and coughed up something onto his pillow. Shivering, expecting disaster, he turned on the bedlight and saw a small ball of blood on the pillow, like a Christmas ornament.

He woke Timmons and asked him to get help and soon the doctor was looking down on him from a great height. Competent, arrogant, he said, "That time bomb we were talking about has just blown up on you. And we don't like blood on the outside. So we're going to take a look inside and pull out the rest of the bomb."

Kathie appeared with a wheelchair and helping him into it said, "We're finally getting some action." She wheeled him onto the deck to get to the operating room. The ship was pitching violently and those by the rail were trying to keep from tossing up. The waves splashed high and several GIs caught the spray and rubbed it on their faces. Outside the operating room GIs were recovering from surgery, sitting on benches like tourists. One lanky soldier in a wheelchair moaned every time the ship rocked and a friend propped him up with a pillow. Somebody said the infirmary had run out of painkillers.

They pushed Richard up to the operating table and from the way the nurses eyed him he figured the operation would fix the problem or put him away. Four arms lifted him onto the table and the doctor stared down on him, his eyes shining above the mask. Waving an X-ray like a flag he said to his assistants, "You can see this tiny bomb in the lung. It entered here in this vein, then took a side trip to the lung. See where it is, right where X marks the spot. We're going to carve him from the side, round the back and up the front, the way you open a can of beans. Then we take half of his lung out and leave him the rest to breathe with."

The sea banged the ship from side to side as if it would rip it apart. "I wouldn't operate in this sea," the doctor said, "if it wasn't an emergency." He looked down onto Richard's face. "I hope you realize, young fellow, I'm making medical history, performing a lobectomy in a storm at sea. It's not easy. So keep your hands out of my face, Kathie, and we'll fix this fellow up for you."

The anesthetist prepared the needle and stood beside the table, with Kathie hovering over Richard.

"Don't get my patient aroused," the doctor said to her.

"Hi, Rich," she said. "Don't mind him. He's got a sick sense of humor. But he'll cut that shrapnel out of you with one stroke. I told him I wanted a first-class carving job."

He felt the needle go into his arm and immediately he was falling down into the swirling whirlpool of a huge water pipe, hearing the humming sound of rushing water. As the dream state came on, he said, "I ask questions, and I want answers."

"What's he muttering about?" the doctor asked.

"Here we go," she said, holding him fast to the table.

"Get your hands out of the patient," the doctor said.

"How are you doing, Rich?" she asked.

"I'm going to fly high and die high."

191

"What's he talking about?" the doctor asked.

"Keep talking," she said.

"I ask questions," he whispered, "and I want answers."

"Remember," Kathie said, "you're at the bottom. You've got nowhere to go but up."

He smiled and disappeared, spinning down into the churning water of the whirlpool, still hearing the monotonous humming sound, feeling high and dizzy as he faded away far into the bottomless tunnel of spiraling water.

Later Kathie was looking down at him, eclipsing the burning operation lights. "It's over," she called to him, holding up a piece of steel the size of her thumb. "Here's your souvenir."

He slept for a long time and dreamt he was standing by his mother's bed. "I haven't much longer," she said. "Waiting for you to come back has been the death of me." His father stood by the bed like a defeated knight in a tapestry. She was going peacefully and wanted to say something to Richard but the drug kept her from speaking. A nurse was combing his mother's hair. Though frail and gaunt his mother was still the young woman he'd taken on that idyllic swim by the lake. She thrust her hand out of the sheets to touch husband or son, whoever would say *bon voyage* as she set off. His father withdrew to the back of the room and Richard didn't have the guts to take his place. "I'm going on a journey," she said, and slipped away. Her face turned to stone.

He woke in the morning from his deep sleep. An ex-POW next to him in the recovery room was groaning. When the man gave him a moment of silence in the early hours, a cleaning woman began polishing the hall with a swirling brush, moving furiously from side to side as if to sweep the universe free of bugs.

Half-awake he walked out onto the deck and took a chair by the railing. GIs sat in wheelchairs, smoking, sleeping, staring out to sea. They seemed proud of their newly acquired skill of staring for hours at nothing. A violent banging shook him and the ship rolled back and forth as if the ocean would turn it over. The spray lashed his face and he looked down from his deck chair at the foam churned up by the wind like the snow at the front. A light came on in his room behind him; someone moved about, then opened the door to the deck, and came out. He slid down in his deck chair.

"Richard," Kathie said. "What are you doing out here? You're wet. Come in." She led him back and once inside took off his bathrobe, dried him off and dressed him in a new hospital gown.

"I must've walked in my sleep. I have something to show you." Reaching under his pillow, he brought out the gift he'd bought in Le Havre.

"What is it?"

"A sitatunga. It can sleep underwater."

She took the brooch with its bright stones. "It's terrific. Who did you buy it for?"

"For you."

"Thanks. But I'm mad at you for going out on deck. And you're not going to sleep underwater. The doctor said he got all the fragments out of your chest. You're a new man."

"Will you put that in your article?"

"Of course."

"Could I see what you've written so far?"

"Sure."

"Did you write about Timmy?"

"No, I couldn't. He's not ready to talk about what happened to him. But I can tell the world what happened to you. Your story will make you famous."

She got the article from her cabin and gave it to him.

On board the Aquitania I met Richard Glasgow, a veteran on his way home from the war.

193

He told me of his harrowing experience in the Ardennes Woods, in the winter of '44.

His division, ill-trained for combat, was wiped out in a couple of weeks, and Richard, severely wounded by fire from a German Tiger tank, was captured by enemy forces.

The warehouse where he was taken with the wounded was bombed by our B-17s and Richard was buried in the ruins.

Then finally with the aid of a French prisoner Richard made a miraculous escape and joined the Russian forces which liberated Domburg, the town where he had been a prisoner.

Richard weathered the storm of war because he had a mission – to help rid the world, he said, of the madman Hitler.

Though the Supreme Command never anticipated the German offensive, Richard kept the faith.

"You can't predict," he said, "what will happen in a war."

Also his love for a beautiful young woman from his hometown kept him from despair during his ordeal.

I'm sure Richard Glasgow will make a successful return to civilian life. The Post honors him for his courageous effort to repel Hitler's last desperate attack on the American forces in the Ardennes woods.

"What do you think of the article?" she asked when he'd finished reading.

"I guess you've got all the facts," he said.

Later in the day he sat in a wheelchair staring with the others at the land coming into view. The sea had calmed down and he drank in the cool offshore breeze.

"We'll be coming into Hampton Roads," Kathie said, adjusting his pin on the pocket of her uniform. Weak from the operation, he couldn't keep back the tears.

The ship slid forward inch by inch until it touched the dock. The GIs and ex-POWs stood at the rails, packs on their backs like mules, straining their heads, burying their eyes in the shore.

Several dockworkers were sunning themselves on the boards of the wharf. Timmons could see a highway in the distance with hundreds of car lights coming on at dusk, shooting in and out like atoms.

Two Red Cross ladies arrived at the wharf carrying baskets, sidestepping the "dead men" as the GIs called the homeless lying on the boards. The taller, holding a white cat on one arm, shouted at the men on the ship, "Welcome home, fellows" and a soldier hollered down, "Thank you, mutha."

The women took their positions on the gangplank as a welcome committee, tiptoed over the mud puddles as to protect their shoes, and pulled down their broad straw hats to shade their eyes from the hot sun. The shorter woman took out a flask from her purse and passed it to her friend who took a swallow. Swaying like a musical-comedy leading lady, the tall one approached the ship and called up to the men, "Hello, boys." A GI bored with the long delay in going ashore shouted, "How much, mutha?"

"No charge for you, son," the tall one said.

She and her partner went to a wall on the dock and picked up a wooden sign with the words *Welcome Home*. Straining to hold it up they stumbled along. Thrown off balance by the weight of the sign the tall woman had to put it down.

The short woman, aware that the men were bored by the delay, took a doughnut from her basket and hurled it playfully toward the GIs at the rails. A hand reached for the prize, which fell back into the water. She threw a second and a third without success. A GI shouted to her, "Come on, mutha, put it over the plate."

Richard leaned out of the wheelchair and reached for one of the flying doughnuts but missed it. A second time he caught one but it fell out of his hand and dropped back into the harbor. Getting the range the tall woman threw one that a GI caught and he lobbed it right back so the Red Cross lady had to duck and the men laughed.

A GI went down to the mess hall and brought up a new batch of doughnuts for ammunition, handing them out to the troops at the railing. Soon doughnuts were sailing down from all along the ship's side like bullets, ricocheting off the boards on the wharf, some falling on the slumbering drifters. One, wakened by the barrage, looked around and without getting up stretched his hand for a stray doughnut, dusted off the dirt and ate it.

Spurred on by the battle a leader of the GIs near Richard – a short man with a harelip – spun a doughnut across the wharf like a stone off the water and caught the foot of the short woman. He fired another, a fat jelly doughnut, which hit the tall one on the head, making her jump and slide on the wet wharf as she bobbed out of the way, clutching her cat.

A hail of hard stale doughnuts enveloped the short woman, a few hitting her on the back. Frightened, she rushed off to join her friend and the two scurried off to the road back to town. Mad at the delay in disembarking, the embittered leader shouted at the women, "Go back to your cathouse."

Richard wheeled up to the man, "Why are you firing at them, asshole?"

"How can they welcome thousands of GIs with a basket of doughnuts?"

"You're a hero. You deserve a medal."

The fellow cursed him and moved along down the railing.

Timmons realized the GIs were losing hope. They felt they'd never move down the gangplank. Some demon officer must've overslept and forgot to give the order for the trucks. The dark mood of the camps swept over him.

He heard the preacher's voice coming over the loudspeaker, "When Christ screamed on the cross, He didn't understand. Later He realized He had suffered to give us eternal life. When we were bombed by our own men we screamed and didn't understand. But God has His reasons. Someday we will see clearly what today we only see in a glass darkly."

The GIs listened with reverence, but Timmons smiled. So, he thought, there was a meaning to life – you just couldn't find it. Everything that's screwed up would be explained later. Maybe the war would've turned out the same for them even if their outfit had been prepared. Something always went wrong in combat. You couldn't predict where the shells would fall.

He stared at the land. He'd been held up long enough. He wanted to get back into the traffic and become part of the congestion.

"Rich," he asked his friend, "what am I going to do when I get back?"

"You'll want to get a job, I guess. I can ask dad to find a position for you in the steel plant. They'll need people this summer."

"I won't want to work for a while. I have to get my head clear. You see those cars? Those drivers shooting in and out of town have forgotten there ever was a war. We're already a footnote in some book – 'nine thousand GIs were lost somewhere in the Ardennes.' Nobody will remember it unless they read an old newspaper being tossed out with the garbage. But this war nearly destroyed me. Our General led us against thousands of *Volksgrenadiers*, knowing many guys had never fired their guns. And then he snuck away to Paris to call himself a war hero. Even Eisenhower figured the Germans would never attack us, and when they did, he was having a party."

"Well, he had the enormous responsibility for this war thrust on him. He's a human being – he made a mistake. And he admitted it. He was also a lonely man – his wife was far away in the States. Why couldn't he have a little celebration?"

"But we weren't having any party."

"Timmy, I think you're missing something. I'll never forget that short young girl behind the barbed wire, with black skin, her hair shaved off, stripped to the waist, in that ridiculous black-and-white striped pants like Charlie Chaplin, looking about with haunted eyes, as if she'd been chased by devils."

"I can't bear to think about it."

"At least we tried to rid the world of a madman who was burning his own people."

"You're crazy, Richard. We didn't do a damn thing. How long will you go on deluding yourself?"

Kathie came up to Richard on the deck, as he waited for disembarkment, feeling the cooling effects of the whirling sea spray on his face.

"I've been on this shuttle for a year," she said. "And I know who's going to make it and who won't."

"I hope Timmy makes it."

"There's a saying about your friend –'you can drown close to shore too.' As for you, 'the world's your oyster, so eat it.'"

"I wonder what I'll think about everything that happened."

"Well, as the saying goes, 'Why worry about tomorrow when today's so far away?'"

"Stop quoting. What do you really think? You've seen so many coming home to a strange new world."

"Look at this," she said, taking out a seashell from her purse. "Now shut your eyes and hold it to your ear." He did as she suggested. "Now," she went on, "do you hear a sound like waves far away?" He nodded yes. "Well," she concluded, "according to my book, that's your soul whispering to you from the shore of the unknown."

He put his arm on her shoulder. He'd hold on to her for the

short time they'd be together – a life buoy thrown down to all the drowning men.

He thought again about all that had happened. Had he passed the test? He remembered the story of Lancelot he read in college – who went through violent trials but failed in his quest and only had a faint glimpse of the Grail.

Well, he felt like singing. He could see again and he was going home – and to loved ones who thought they were heroes.

As the nurse said, quoting her book – "The streets of home might still be as bright as the paths of heaven."

About the Author

Donald Young taught Creative Writing at Williams College in Massachusetts and at Cabrillo College in California. He gave a course on English Drama in London for the American Institute of Foreign Studies.

He has published poetry in *Epoch, Western Review*, and *The Texas Review,* as well as in other literary magazines.

His first published novel was *The Reunion.*

Books of poetry include *The Shore of the Unknown, Illumination, Reflections, New Vistas, Sonnets on Shakespeare* and the collected poems, *The Invisible Harbor.*

Donald Young lives in Aptos, California.